The Baker's Memory

The Baker's Memory

EMILY ECHOLS

1000 Cedars Press

To my grandmothers,
Dorothy Smith and Mary Nell Benson

The power of population is so superior to the power of the earth to produce subsistence for man, that premature death must in some shape or other visit the human race.

-Thomas Malthus

CHAPTER 1

Some days Maureen thought about escaping. She didn't have a plan. She had no means of transportation. Her understanding of geography was so limited that she didn't have a name for the place she would go. She had a difficult time imaging another world. Still, this cloudy idea would rise to the surface like a bubble when she had a terrible day, on days like this one. It was a fragile idea that was easily dispelled.

The stale, humid air sucked the life out of Maureen's dream. She walked slowly, trying to keep her movements to a minimum, hoping to produce less sweat. Her pale yellow coveralls clung to her. She twisted her thick curly dark hair off her neck and into a ponytail. It stuck in her fingers. She hoped they would approve new summer uniforms soon. Then she shook the thought away. New summer uniforms had been rumored for years. They probably weren't going to ever happen.

Maureen walked two more blocks past pastel-colored apartment buildings with Spanish tile roofs. She walked past a store selling sheets, towels and other small household items. Maureen didn't know anyone wealthy enough to shop there. She shook her head at the kiosk that sold shoelaces and copied keys. She thought it had to be a front for something. There was no way anyone made a living selling shoelaces and copying keys.

Maureen walked into Sally's Bar and sat at their usual table in the back corner. It was only mildly cooler inside, probably because it was darker. The front windows were propped open and overhead fans tried to circulate the steamy air. Their usual waitress walked by and nodded hello to Maureen.

Maureen wondered how other people lived. What was life like outside of Harvest? She wondered which parts of the world had recovered from The Collapse and which parts were still devastated. She wondered if there were large populations that were sustained by farming, maybe on the other side of the world. She tried to come up with a name for a place to escape to. No matter how hard she thought, the only faraway place name she could remember was Eden but that didn't sound right.

Maybe things wouldn't be so bad if she had a different job. She knew that the CDT, the Career Decision Test they all took after high school, was in place to help them. The CDT had begun as a Jasper Industries recruiting tool but it proved so reliable that its use expanded until it was a requirement for all graduating high school seniors. Maureen knew that she had the skills and the talents to be a great preschool teacher. She just hated it. She knew she wasn't supposed to hate it. She didn't really understand why she did since she was a skilled preschool teacher.

Maureen knew that, though the CDT helped most people there seemed to be a small minority that was unhappy in their current occupation because they had dreamed of doing something different. The CDT didn't accommodate dreams. In the back of her mind she felt like she was designed for greater things. It was like her thought about wanting to leave. She didn't know where it came from or what to do with it so she tried not to dwell on it, instead burying it deep inside her.

"Maureen!" Bernadette squealed, bounding into the bar. She gave her a warm hug and sat on the stool opposite Maureen. Bernadette's gold hair flipped out on the ends. Maureen was fairly certain that particular style was no longer approved but Bernadette had been wearing her hair that way for as long as she could remember. "How are you?"

"OK," Maureen responded, "You?"

"Things have been kind of slow at Dr. F's but they try to keep me busy," Bernadette answered cheerfully. She studied Maureen's face and frowned. "You seem kind of down. Are you really OK?"

"Yeah," Maureen paused, looking at Bernadette's pale green coveralls and said quietly, "Do you like your job?"

"I am very competent at what I do." Bernadette's response was textbook.

"Yes, I know you're good at it but do you *like* it? Do you *enjoy* it?" Maureen prodded.

"Maureen, are you OK? Have you been...reading again?" Bernadette whispered "reading" like it was a dirty word.

"No, I haven't been reading again," Maureen sighed. "I still have another month to go before the suspension ends."

"Oh thank goodness! I was so worried that you'd been reading again and that's what this was all about. I mean, I can't believe you got so worked up over a silly book."

"Silly book?! *Wuthering Heights* is not a silly book!" Maureen's voice rose and she started to stand. *"Wuthering Heights* is a beautiful book! And it changed me! And I just wanted to share it but then..."

"Maureen!" Bernadette cut her off and Maureen returned to her seat. "That is enough!" Bernadette gestured around the bar to indicate they were in a public place. People were staring.

Maureen lowered her head. "That's not the point," she began again, speaking into her chest. "I was just wondering how you felt about your job."

"Sweetie, it's not really about how we *feel* about our jobs, now is it? I'm good at what I do and I have the right temperament for it. And it's the same for you. Where's all this nonsense about liking our jobs coming from?"

"Before The Collapse people got to choose their jobs. Sometimes I wish I lived during the Golden Age of Food," Maureen mumbled.

"You don't know what you're saying. We were in the same food history class. The whole system was too unstable. Some people were overweight while other people starved to death. The population was out of control. We just ran out of resources. It wasn't sustainable and Jasper Industries has proven over and over again that it's still not."

"But doesn't it seem like people might have been, I don't know, happier?"

"Happier? Because food-borne illness and starvation makes people cheerful?"

"I've been thinking." Maureen leaned across the table excitedly. "Don't you think we're missing something without food, I mean more than food? Don't you think we lost...cultural memory or table fellowship or something?"

"Cultural memory? What is with you today? Is this because you heard about Matthew?"

A waitress brought menus to the table and the conversation paused. Bernadette told the waitress, "I'll have the usual but could you add a little Sarsaparilla root to help me unwind?" The waitress nodded and turned to Maureen.

"I'd just like a Pink," she said.

As the waitress left, Bernadette scowled at Maureen. "Why do you always order that? I heard they're going to discontinue colors soon. It's so stupid.

Why would anyone want to drink pink H_2O?"

"I don't know. I like it. It makes me smile," she answered. Bernadette dropped the subject.

"Heard what about Matthew? Matthew Miller?" Maureen asked.

"Yeah, I saw Louisa a few days ago. She told me that she heard from June that Matthew Miller is a..." Bernadette paused. She glanced around the bar dramatically. She leaned in closer to Maureen and whispered, "a Foodie." She looked around the bar again to see if anyone had heard.

"Matthew Miller? A Foodie?" Maureen exclaimed.

"Keep it down!" Bernadette hissed. She actually seemed worried this time.

"Do you know where he is?"

"No! I don't know where he is! And you don't want to know either. The last thing you need is to get involved with Foodies," Bernadette scolded. She paused and a sly smile came across her face, "Is this because you had a crush on him in high school? Do you want to find him because you're in *love* with him?"

Maureen ignored that last comment. "You know, there's no way they're really as bad as the news says."

"Not so bad, huh? What about those Foodies who tried to blow up the Jasper Industries building? They seem pretty dangerous to me."

"But that was just one group. I don't think all Foodies are violent. Besides, I think there have to be way more of them than the media says."

"For one, there can't be that many of them. Large scale farming simply isn't possible anymore. And two, we shouldn't even be talking about this. I just thought it was good gossip that Matthew Miller turned into one since he was your high school love and all."

"He was not." Maureen paused thoughtfully, "Sometimes I think I'd like to try food."

"Maureen, are you crazy? Don't you know how dangerous food consumption is these days?"

The waitress interrupted Bernadette's speech by bringing drinks. They both dutifully removed the small EZ Meal pellets from one of the many pockets in their color-coded coveralls and took them with their H_2O. Maureen knew that the food coloring didn't affect the flavor of the H_2O but she was convinced that it made it taste better.

"Aren't you curious about the Foodies?" Maureen began again after a few moments of silence while they finished Third Meal. "Don't you wonder what they're like? Do you ever wonder what food tasted like?"

"No, I don't!" Bernadette snapped. "The system failed, Maureen. I will take my EZ Meal three times a day like every other sane person on the planet, thank you very much. I really don't have time for your conspiracy theories today. So, no I don't ever wonder what it would be like to be a Foodie!" Bernadette took a breath and continued more calmly, "We shouldn't even be having this conversation. We could both lose our traveling privileges."

Maureen couldn't let it die just yet. "What is it with you and traveling privileges? You're always threatening that when I say things you don't like. Well you know what? I don't care! I never travel anyway!" Maureen stood suddenly and walked to the restroom. She splashed cold water on her face and stared at herself in the mirror. Her ears were red. They always got red when she was angry and people always felt the need to point it out to her, which just made her angrier. She pressed her sweaty hands against her hot ears, waiting for the ringing to stop. She closed her eyes and took a deep breath.

This had been happening more and more often. It was why Bernadette felt the need to try to censor her, to remind her they were in public and people could hear their conversation. This was what happened with *Wuthering Heights* and this was why she wasn't allowed back in the library. Maureen had lost her filter when her parents died. She was a teenager then so people accepted it and acted like it was OK. Only, it wasn't OK and as she lost control of her temper her lack of a verbal filter was becoming dangerous. Unlike nearly everyone else in Harvest, Maureen said exactly what she was thinking. Someday she might lose more than her library privileges or her traveling privileges. Maureen turned the faucet back on and lowered her face into the cool stream. One day saying whatever she thought might get her killed.

Maureen pulled her face up. The curls around her face were wet. Maureen toweled off her face and washed her sweaty hands slowly. She knew it was a problem. She'd been this way for years and didn't know how to fix it. Words just spilled out of her mouth without her consent. She lost control of the volume of her voice. She said hurtful things to her only friend. Maureen took one more deep breath and returned to the table intending to apologize to Bernadette.

"Sweetie, I'm so sorry I got you so worked up. It was all my fault. Forgive me?" Bernadette rattled off her apology before Maureen even sat down. Bernadette always did the apologizing. Maureen knew she should too but she couldn't quite form the words. She didn't know how to apologize for feeling deeply and thinking critically. She never apologized for her outbursts.

Maureen smiled a half smile. "It's OK," she replied meekly. They retreated to safer topics. They talked about Bernadette's brother's recent CDT results (veterinarian) and Louisa's new baby (a boy who wasn't sleeping).

Maureen let her mind wander while Bernadette told detailed stories about Louisa's new baby. How could there be so many stories about a newborn baby? Maureen had heard all the points that Bernadette made about the Foodies on the news just like everyone else. Only, Maureen didn't exactly believe it all. Wasn't it in Jasper Industries best interests to continue reporting that traditional farming wasn't possible? They continued to report poor soil quality, droughts and extreme weather all over the globe. They even went so far as to say that the lack of skilled labor was enough of a deterrent to prevent traditional farming from ever returning. Dr. James Jasper developed EZ Meal as a solution to a crisis. Maureen wondered if the crisis would ever be over.

As they were departing Bernadette gave Maureen a hug that made it difficult for her to breathe.

"Sweetie, I worry about you sometimes. Please tell me if you need anything or if you're in real trouble." Maureen gasped for air as Bernadette let her go.

"I'm fine. Really. But I do appreciate the offer." She tried to sound calm. Bernadette seemed placated, nodded goodbye and they parted.

CHAPTER 2

Maureen couldn't stop thinking about Matthew Miller and the Foodies. When she returned to her sparse, dark apartment she carried a single cardboard box out of her closet. She pulled out some family photos, flipping through them. She stared at the smiling faces in a photo of her, her brother Sam, her mother and father standing in front of the apartment she grew up in. They all squinted into the sun and looked like they were on the verge of laughter. Maureen couldn't remember what had been so funny or even who took the photograph. It was a distant life. She stuffed the photographs back in the box.

Finally, she pulled out a tattered spiral-bound notebook. Maureen had read library books voraciously her entire life and this spiral held the culmination of her studies. Maureen ran her finger down the lists she had painstakingly made. It might have looked like chaos to anyone else but all the notes and cross-references made sense to her. It was Maureen's book of food. When she read, if she came upon a reference to food or a description of food, she wrote it down in this notebook. It was filled with foods she had no reference point for. What does this look like? Taste like? Did this food hold meaning for people? She'd tried to categorize food by which meal it was eaten at, if it was meat, or a fruit or a vegetable or a grain. Sometimes this was difficult because the authors who took food for granted didn't often provide many details. But through years of reading and careful research, Maureen had an extensive list.

Maureen thought there should be food historians, keeping this history alive but it seemed that most people wanted to put that past behind them. No one alive today had ever eaten so most people didn't understand. Truly, Maureen didn't either. But, through reading, she knew that many important conversations seemed to happen around a table, food was central to celebrations, and that different places and cultures had eaten different food. It seemed important. Since no one else seemed to be doing the legwork, Maureen took it upon herself.

The suspension of her library privileges had slowed her research. Maureen knew that before The Collapse there had been personal libraries. The idea was delicious and dangerous to her. After The Collapse books were rounded up to save them, to share them. With the death of the publishing industry, like so much else, there was a shortage of books. Maureen flipped through the pages of her notebook. She wondered if Matthew had tasted all of this food, if they were even able to procure the ingredients for all of these foods.

Maureen got off the floor and lifted herself onto the kitchen counter. Her apartment was just one large room. She slept on the foldout couch in the living room. She had one closet and a small bathroom. Even though the kitchen wasn't a separate room it felt different to Maureen and she did her best thinking in there. She untied her boots and let them fall to the ground. She swung her legs, knocking her heels against the wooden cabinets. The thumping helped to clear her mind. She looked at her oven and range. The gas to the building was disconnected but the oven still sat in its cubbyhole in the kitchen. She even still had a refrigerator. It wasn't plugged in and if she had plugged it in she wouldn't be able to afford the electricity to keep it running. People weren't concerned about removing appliances in such low-rent apartments. Maureen scanned her food list, making mental notes of how she thought different dishes were cooked. Oven. On the stove. Oven. Matthew.

Maureen sighed loudly and stopped kicking the cabinets. She sat very still, trying to collect herself but it didn't work. She started to sob. Matthew and Bernadette were her only real friends from high school. Maureen had a breakdown after her parents died. Her teachers cut her so much slack that she barely had to do anything to graduate. Sometimes Maureen wondered if she should blame being a preschool teacher on her own grades those last few years instead of the CDT.

Maureen had always felt fragile, different from other people. Losing her parents ripped a gaping hole inside of her, a hole that Maureen still didn't know how to close. So she turned the feelings outward. She started to lose her temper. Her teachers whispered about her "acting out" but Maureen knew it was more than that. Matthew and Bernadette stood up for her and protected her. She and Matthew had spent a lot of time alone talking.

She remembered sitting with him in Jasper Park near the end of their senior year, talking about their hopes for their CDT results. Matthew wanted to be a doctor. Maureen wanted to do something creative even though there were few sanctioned artist jobs anymore. She'd said something to make him laugh and he'd put his hand on her knee. Maureen remembered the electricity shooting through her body. Usually she was estimating the inches between their feet, their shoulders. She was thrilled by this small touch.

They'd talked about how parents and teachers kept telling them to watch their expectations. They didn't want them to be disappointed. One could not always predict CDT results. But how do you tell an eighteen-year-old not to dream?

Occupations were highly segregated. CDT results often ended friendships. Maureen had expressed concern that they wouldn't be friends anymore. Matthew said that no matter what, they always would be.

It seemed like a silly promise, a juvenile promise, and one that would be hard to keep. For some reason, coming from Matthew, Maureen believed it. She had to. Matthew was the only person she could really talk to and Maureen didn't know what she would do without him. She couldn't imagine how lonely her life would be without him so she chose to believe his promise.

After high school, she stayed in touch with Bernadette mostly out of Bernadette's persistence. There were days she wasn't even very fond of her. If it had solely been up to Maureen to keep in touch she probably wouldn't have any friends at all. Maureen wanted to change but making the decision didn't seem to change her personality. Sometimes Maureen felt she'd end up all alone in every way.

Now Matthew was a Foodie and in Maureen's mind that seemed perfect. It seemed like the perfect place for him, at least in the way that Maureen imagined the Foodies. Maureen thought the Foodies sounded romantic, living off the land like their ancestors. It sounded so poetic. They grew all their own food and kept animals just like people did in the twentieth century, the Golden Age of Food.

As much as she romanticized the Foodies, they also terrified her. Some of them did blow up buildings. A lot of secrecy surrounded them. Maureen knew some of it was for their protection. For the most part, Jasper Industries tried to deny their existence, saying that it still wasn't possible to grow food citing statistics about fertilizer and soil. What frightened and thrilled her the most about them was the prospect of eating food. She had been taught that growing food was primitive; obviously it hadn't worked out. Maureen dreamt about food often but she didn't feel brave enough to leave Harvest.

Maureen sniffled and wiped her face on her sleeve. She jumped down from the counter and stuffed her food notebook back in the box. She hid it away in the closet. The threadbare couch squeaked as she sat down. She tried to count the days until her library privileges returned. She could make it. She wasn't sure how she had made it so long without books already. She promised herself that never again would she do something to endanger her right to read, no matter how the books stirred her soul.

She walked to the window and searched the night sky. She wondered where Matthew and the Foodies were, what they were doing. Were they enjoying food around a table? Maureen let out a ragged sigh. She ached for something she'd never known.

CHAPTER 3

The next morning Maureen walked to Jasper Park to meet her bother, Sam. A slight breeze made it feel like a glorious spring day instead of the dead of summer. Maureen walked past the peach, yellow and pink apartment buildings with Spanish tile roofs. As she crossed the street, she was forced to step out of the shade and into the sun. It no longer felt like spring. Maureen secretly wished she could wear a hat as she squinted into the sun. As she neared the only park in town she could see Sam waiting for her. She smiled at her tall, blonde brother, the antithesis of herself. He'd brought his golden retriever, Cookie, and a ball to throw for her.

"How's the factory?" Maureen asked after they hugged hellos.

Sam rubbed the back of his crew cut blonde head. "It's good. There's some talk of new products, which has everyone freaking out but I think its just rumor. They're always saying that." Sam paused, "Everything OK with you?"

"I'm OK. Work sucks, as usual. Oh! I do have some news. Bernadette told me that Matthew Miller, remember him from my class?"

"Isn't that the guy you were madly in love with?" Sam asked, barely stifling a laugh.

"Yeah, that's the guy but I wasn't in love with him. Fine, whatever I liked him. Anyway, Bernadette told me that he's a," she glanced around just like Bernadette had. There were some mothers and children on the playground about two hundred feet away. There were some joggers on the track around the duck pond. No one was within earshot. "A Foodie," she finally finished.

"Huh. A Foodie? I wouldn't have pegged him for one."

"That's it? That's your reaction? Aren't you shocked or interested or excited?"

"Nah, not really. I hear about the Foodies all the time from Travis."

"Wait, what? How does Travis know about the Foodies?"

"He works for them. Sometimes."

"Hold up. What do you mean 'he works for them'? Works for them how?" Maureen collapsed onto a wooden bench behind them. Sam threw the ball for Cookie again and joined her on the bench.

"You know how Travis drives that truck to work? Well, sometimes, he transports stuff for the Foodies. They pay him. They even feed him sometimes."

"Where are they? How does he know them? What does he transport for them? What's food like?"

"Hold it," Sam interrupted. "I only know what Travis has told me and it's not much. He doesn't want to lose his truck, he doesn't want the Foodies to be found by the authorities and he especially doesn't want to disappear. All I know is: Every few weeks, maybe once a month, they contact him and ask him to transport some goods. Sometimes he picks up supplies for them. Whatever they've asked him to do. And he does it and they pay him. Once, they invited him to stay for Third Meal. Sometimes they give him sweets. That's really all I know. I don't know where they are or anything. Travis won't tell me—I've asked."

"Why does he do that for them? Why can't they do it themselves?"

"Most of them are unregistered so they can't move freely. Travis says they look different than we do, too. He says the women wear skirts and dresses, real old-fashioned stuff. But Travis says the women are more beautiful. He says there's something different about them, healthier."

"It's not possible to be healthier than we are. We're supposed to be the healthiest generation ever."

"I don't know. He said it was hard to explain. I swear that's all I know."

Maureen was lost in thought. Her mind was humming with possibilities. "Can you give me Travis's phone number?"

"No, I can't. The last thing you need is to get wrapped up in all of this. You're close to getting your library privileges back. I promise everything will look better when you're allowed to read again. Don't go looking for trouble. I know you were in love with Matthew in high school but it's just not worth it."

"Ugh! This isn't about Matthew. I'm just curious. Please?"

"I can't. No, I won't. As long as you're still going on about Mom and Dad disappearing instead of being dead, I can't tell you how to contact Travis."

"Where'd that come from? Have you been talking to Bernadette? I haven't said that in a long time! I'm just saying we never saw the bodies! That's all. I just wish we could have seen them." As Maureen finished, her voice trailed off into a sad little girl voice.

"Look, I'm sorry. I shouldn't have brought them up. I just don't want you to get into any more trouble, that's all. I worry about you sometimes."

"Damn it! Losing my library privileges for six months is hardly real trouble. What do I have to do to keep people from worrying about me?"

"Stop being you," Sam smiled and winked at her. "I should take Cookie home. I've got to get to work. Be careful, Little Sister."

"I love you too," Maureen said as they embraced and Maureen scratched Cookie's head. "See you guys later."

As Maureen walked to work, being careful to walk in the shade, she realized how many questions she had for Travis. How did the Foodies find him? Where did they live? How were they different? What was food like? That last one was the biggest question. Travis had actually eaten food; something that most people had never done in their lives. Maureen tried to imagine tall, gangly, fire-haired Travis sitting at a table, sharing a meal with Foodies. Sam said he even ate sweets sometimes. Travis had all his teeth and seemed healthy enough. Maybe he was lying about the sweets to impress Sam. From what Maureen remembered about Travis that seemed likely. Not that Travis was a liar, he just tended to embellish his stories a bit. Sam underestimated Maureen. Travis wouldn't be too hard to find.

Maureen wished that information were easier to come by. For many years the lack of information could be chalked up to uncertainty. It was many years after The Collapse before there was any kind of government and even longer before the government was able to organize a census. That meant that for years they really didn't know how many people survived, let alone whom. It should have been simpler now. Everyone was required to be registered. Maureen glanced down at the emblem of wheat beside her nameplate, the sign that she was registered. She knew it was possible to counterfeit nameplates. People also sold them on the black market. Besides the nameplate clearly visible on one's coveralls people were also required to carry their ID cards at all times. They were becoming more and more difficult to counterfeit. They had holograms on them now, which made Maureen feel like she lived in the future.

Since the government kept such a tight watch on everyone, it seemed that information should be more plentiful. The government had the information now but they weren't sharing. Even asking seemingly benign questions, like what a student's parents did for a living, could potentially be classified information. All this secrecy made it difficult to meet new people. You were never sure how much to share with strangers. It made it nearly impossible to find old friends. Everything had to go through your class representative. If you were looking for someone who'd graduated a different year you were out of luck because you didn't have access to that class representative. Maureen sighed. It seemed complicated to have to bribe an official for a friend's phone number but it was the only way Maureen had ever known.

Maureen would have to be creative. Unfortunately that meant asking Bernadette for help, which Maureen hated doing. Bernadette's father was the village magistrate and sometimes her connections with government officials were too good to ignore. Maureen hated asking Bernadette for favors especially because she liked to drop the phrase, "My father, the magistrate," with regularity, as though Maureen might have forgotten. Maureen sighed heavily. She vowed to call Bernadette after work then stopped herself.

Was this really about Foodies or was this about

Matthew? Was there a difference? Maureen tried to decide why she thought she needed to talk to Travis. She also tried to understand Sam's side. Sam was just trying to protect her and it was true that she'd gotten into some minor trouble in the past. But this was different. This was just a conversation. Or was it? What did Maureen think she was going to do with the information that Travis gave her? It came back to Matthew. Would she use what he told her to find Matthew? Maureen couldn't decide.

The last time she'd acted rashly she'd lost her library privileges. She decided she needed some time to think. More than anything she needed a way to distract herself for the next few weeks. She knew what she had to do but dreaded it anyway.

After she got home from work that day, she called Bernadette and asked her about the next Young Citizens Consortium meeting. Bernadette told her they didn't meet for a few weeks but that the Daughters of the Food Revolution were meeting the next day at her apartment. Every muscle on Maureen's face tightened but she said that she'd be there.

CHAPTER 4

The next day, Maureen called Bernadette because she couldn't remember when the Daughters of the Food Revolution meeting was. Bernadette told her to hurry over because her cousin, Herman, was there. Herman interrupted Bernadette to tell her he had to leave. Bernadette told Maureen to hurry over anyway.

When Maureen hung up the phone she banged her head on the rickety kitchen table. A Daughters of the Food Revolution meeting at Bernadette's apartment? She must really be desperate. Thank goodness Cousin Herman had to leave. Bernadette just might have died of happiness if she got to introduce them *and* have her at a DFR meeting. She'd been trying to get them to date for as long as Maureen could remember. She was pretty sure she wasn't interested in anymore named Herman. Or anyone related to Bernadette.

With that thought Maureen pulled herself together and made the quick walk to Bernadette's apartment. Bernadette's apartment always seemed cleaner than Maureen's and it always smelled better. All of Bernadette's furniture was new, matched, and unstained. Apartments were assigned based on a person's job. Bernadette was a receptionist at a doctor's office, not a high-ranking official. Even though her father was the village magistrate it still seemed fishy.

"I just couldn't believe that you wanted to come to a DFR meeting. I thought that wasn't your thing since I invite you all the time and you never want to join in the fun!" Bernadette said as she carried a tray with a metal pitcher of H_2O and several glasses into the room and set it on the coffee table.

"Yeah, well, like I said I need another hobby for at least a few weeks. I thought maybe the..." Maureen cleared her throat as she choked the words out, "I thought the DFR might be fun. You always say such nice things about them."

"It's such a great group of ladies! You're going to love them! And you're going to love the DFR. We do *so much* for the community."

"What have you done lately?"

"Oh well, you know, this and that."

Maureen rolled her eyes just as the doorbell rang and Bernadette went to answer it. Maureen sunk into the plush pink velvet couch. The squeals from the door rattled her nerves. She pet the armrest in an attempt to soothe herself.

"Maureen! Do you remember June Addison from school?" Bernadette asked as she led plain, sweet June Addison into the room. Of course

Maureen remembered her. June and Bernadette had been in charge of every social function in high school. June was the head of the reunion committee, which meant that she was always harassing people for information about their classmates, which Maureen thought must be a cover for trying to learn incriminating information about them. No one was that interested in acquaintances.

"Of course! June, it's so good to see you!" Maureen said, attempting cheerful but sounding more sarcastic than she intended.

"It's great to see you too, Maureen! I'm so glad you finally decided to join the DFR!" June responded, completely oblivious to Maureen's sarcastic tone. Maureen sat on the pink velvet couch while Bernadette and June sat in the floral side chairs that Bernadette had assembled around the coffee table. Maureen caught herself staring at June's plum-colored coveralls, trying to remember what area they stood for. There had been so many changes recently that she couldn't keep the different colors straight. Bernadette answered the question before she could ask it.

"How're the third graders?" Bernadette asked.

"Adorable as ever!" June answered. The doorbell rang and Bernadette excused herself.

By eighteen hundred hours Bernadette's living room was packed with twittering young women. Most of them sat on metal folding chairs Bernadette had arranged around the room. A couple women sat cross legged on the newly-mopped floor. Maureen's head swam with all the new names she'd learned. She leaned into the arm of the pink couch, hoping not to be noticed.

"Ladies, ladies, let's call this meeting of the Daughters of the Food Revolution to order!" Bernadette said after giving everyone two minutes to take Third Meal. "Can you read the minutes from the last meeting?" she asked, turning to an angular petite woman with huge brown eyes who looked permanently surprised.

"Oh yes," the woman began. "Our July second meeting was called to order by our president, Bernadette. Then we read the minutes from the last meeting. We didn't have any old business to discuss. Then we talked about service projects we might like to do. We talked about working in the park and picking up trash. We talked about maybe doing something with children. We also discussed having a big party. I guess all of that's on-going. We didn't make any formal decisions."

"So I guess that's all old business for us to continue discussing. I think a trash pick-up in the park is a great idea. Does someone want to make a motion?" Bernadette asked.

"I'd like to make a motion that we have a party!" a curvy woman named Ethel squealed.

"We were talking about picking up trash," Bernadette said.

"Oh yes, a party! I second that!" the club secretary with large eyes said.

"All in favor?" Ethel asked. Fifteen ladies, every-one but Maureen and Bernadette, said "aye".

"Wait, wait! Ethel! You're out of order! Only I can do the vote," Bernadette whined. "Besides, we were talking about a service project."

"But we already voted for the party," Ethel pro-tested.

Maureen felt her eyes glazing over.

"Fine, fine. We can talk about the party first but then we need to talk about a service project. We are a service club. That's what it says in our charter, any-way," Bernadette said.

The room erupted into squeals and giggles as the women discussed theme ideas for the party. Maureen's head ached from all the squealing. During the party discussion June elbowed Maureen. She whispered, "Come with me to the kitchen." Maureen looked at her, puzzled.

"Ladies, would anyone like a refill?" June asked. Several women held up their glasses.

"Help me, Maureen," June said, as she started col-lecting glasses and shoving them into Maureen's hands.

"Oh, you don't have to do that," Bernadette pro-tested, starting to stand.

"Don't worry about it. We've got it," June said glancing back at Maureen.

June and Maureen carried the glasses, the flow-ered tray and the metal pitcher back into the kitchen.

"Bernadette told me you were interested in Matthew Miller," June said when they were safely behind the white kitchen cabinets. Even though they weren't needed, most apartments still had large old-fashioned kitchens. Many nicer apartments, like Bernadette's had been re-modeled and all the appliances removed.

"I heard he was a Foodie. I was intrigued," Maureen said, unsure where the conversation was going.

"Of course you were! You were so in love with him in high school. He was really cute!"

"How did you hear he defected?"

"Oh, honey. We don't like to call it that. Let's say he joined the Foodies. It sounds less...political. Well, I actually heard from his ex-girlfriend, Denise, she cuts hair down at that salon on Oak. She said that right after they broke up he just disappeared. He'd talked about wanting to join The Foodies so she just assumed he had."

"Just like that? She didn't try to find him or anything?"

"Apparently not. She was already seeing Eddie Alvarez by then anyway. She said she thought he was doing what he'd always wanted."

"Did she say why he joined?"

"I don't know. I was wondering that, too. Why would anyone want to be a Foodie? Denise said he wasn't happy. I can't imagine he'd be happier as a Foodie, though. It's hard to say why anybody does anything..."

Maureen felt the window closing as June filled the remaining glasses with H_2O but she tried to squeeze in one last question.

"Did Denise know where the Foodies were?"

"No, I asked her." Maureen felt the window slam shut. June squeezed Maureen's arm like they were best friends sharing a secret and gave her a big smile. "You'll let me know if you find out more? If he contacts you or something? I'd love to be able to find him for the reunion in a couple years," June added winking.

With that comment Maureen knew that June wasn't just nosy. She must be a Monitor. Usually they weren't as straightforward as June. Maybe June didn't care if Maureen knew her status. Maureen smiled back without showing her teeth.

The rest of the meeting went by in a blur. Maureen couldn't take her eyes off June. She found hidden meaning behind everything June did or said and realized she was terrified to say anything in her presence. Maureen was thankful when the meeting ended.

Once home, Maureen sat at the kitchen table with mismatched chairs, contemplating what she had learned. She was frustrated with her secondhand sources. No one knew anything. Sam wouldn't tell her anything. June didn't know anything. Denise, if Maureen was remembering the right person, wasn't very bright. Like June had said, if Denise were dating Eddie now she wouldn't even care to talk about Matthew. Maureen felt a pang of jealousy. Why had Matthew dated Denise? She was pretty but Denise? If that was the kind of girl he liked there was no way he'd ever been interested in her. But even that realization didn't keep her from wanting to find him.

Now the possibility of joining the Foodies was staring her in the face. She and Matthew had asked some of the same questions and he'd seemed to find an answer. Maureen couldn't begin to know how to find the Foodies even if she did want to join them. But she did want to leave, she knew that much. Then she thought of Sam. Sam would never leave Harvest.

Sam lived in their parents' old apartment. He moved in after their parents died to stay with Maureen. He'd stayed after Maureen had moved out, which seemed fine and normal. What wasn't normal was that he hadn't redecorated. In fact, he hadn't moved anything. He hadn't touched a thing in their parents' bedroom and continued to sleep in his childhood room. He had brought very little from his own apartment. Maureen was secretly convinced that he believed their parents would just come strolling in one day. She'd tried to ask him about it before. He'd said that it looked so nice already why did he need to redecorate? She couldn't convince Sam that it was a problem. Maureen knew he would never leave so she couldn't either.

CHAPTER 5

The next morning Maureen was so frustrated with herself that she decided to cut most of her hair off. At the time it seemed like the only sensible thing to do. She stared at her long thick curly brown hair in the mirror. It was too heavy. It was holding her back. Everything would seem brighter if she had less hair.

She walked the few blocks to the hair salon on Oak and went inside. She was greeted by a busty blonde woman wearing pink coveralls and asked to sit. Maureen studied the poster on the wall, displaying the approved hairstyles. There always seemed to be fewer than last time. She told the woman that she wanted a number six, a shoulder length style. The pretty woman smiled and led her over to the sink to wash her hair.

"You look really familiar," Maureen started.

"You do too. Did we go to high school together or something?" the woman asked.

"We did go to school together. Aren't you Denise Fleming? I'm Maureen Baker." Maureen smiled. Her plan had worked perfectly.

"Oh yeah, you're that girl whose parents died." Maureen didn't respond. "I'm sorry — I didn't mean — "

"It's OK. How have you been?"

"Good. I am very competent and well tempered for this work. And I have a new boyfriend!" Denise started rinsing Maureen's hair. Maureen flinched at the hot water. "Sorry," Denise said as she turned the heat down.

Maureen decided that was her opening. "I heard you're dating Matthew Miller. We were pretty good friends in school. How is he?"

"Oh, we're not dating anymore. He left. I'm dating Eddie Alvarez now."

"What do you mean 'he left'?"

"I don't really know. He didn't say where he was going. Well, maybe he did. He said he needed to get out. I thought if I heard him say that one more time I would break it off myself. Instead, he broke up with me one day and then just disappeared. Between you and me I think he joined the Foodies."

"What makes you say that?"

Denise put a towel around Maureen's head and they walked back to the chair. Denise glanced around the room and lowered her voice.

"He was always a sympathizer. You know the type, always trying to defend them, saying that they're not all terrorists." Denise put a cape around Maureen and got her scissors out. "I guess it's just a hunch. It just seems like something he would do."

"So you weren't surprised?"

"Not really. I always got this feeling that he was-n't telling me everything. Like, he'd be gone all day and I'd ask where he was and he'd say 'work'. But I totally knew his work hours and knew that wasn't true. But he didn't seem to want me to know so I never asked. I guess most girls would have thought he was cheating but I never thought that."

"So where do you think he went?"

"You know, I can't be sure but I thought he knew Foodies. I think he was somehow involved with them before. That's why I think he left and joined them. This one time, this guy, his name was Anthony," she paused, searching for his last name, "Plumber! He was a huge guy. He came looking for Matt at my apartment. We didn't live together or nothing so I thought it was weird. When I asked him about it later he said he was a friend but he didn't seem too friendly to me."

"So you think maybe this Anthony Plumber was somehow involved with the Foodies?"

"I dunno. Probably. He gave me the creeps. Matt's great and all but I didn't mind so much when he left. We dated for a long time but we weren't happy, you know? I don't think I was what he wanted. And apparently Harvest wasn't either."

Maureen watched inches of her hair fall to the floor. It looked worse when she surveyed the damage on the floor. It was so much hair. Maureen panicked, worrying that she'd done the wrong thing. Denise must have sensed her unease and like a seasoned hairstylist said, "You know, you have really thick hair. So it looks like I'm cutting a ton when you look at the hair on the floor but I promise I'm not cutting that much." Maureen inhaled deeply and calmed down. "You know, now that I think of it, Matt talked about you sometimes."

"Really? What did he say?"

"Just that y'all were great friends. He said you were the best friend he ever had and that he regretted not keeping up with you. So I'd say it wasn't too late. That busy body June probably knew where you were but he'd just say it was a long time ago. Not that long ago, right?"

Maureen smiled. "Sometimes it feels like forever. I'm sorry he's gone."

"I'm not. Don't misunderstand. I miss him but I just think he needed to leave and I hope that he's happy there with them or wherever he is. And I hope the news is wrong about them and that they treat him right, you know?"

"Yeah," Maureen agreed, glad to hear that Matthew might be happier but disappointed that Denise didn't give her much to go on.

"Hey, you know what? Since your hair's so curly and thick I think I'll add in some layers so it's not a total pouf ball. If a Monitor ever asks you, you can say you didn't know your hairstylist *whose name your forgot* did it. It'll look great. And," Denise paused, "it's the least I can do since you were Matt's friend."

Maureen had no idea what Denise was going to

do to her hair but it sounded like a nice thing so she said, "Thanks."

Denise launched into a story about something funny that happened to her boyfriend, Eddie, at work. It sounded like someone had made a mistake but someone else got blamed for it. Maureen's brain was spinning a mile a minute. She couldn't figure out why this was supposed to be a funny story. She was too busy trying to decide whether she should search for Anthony Plumber. Maybe there was a Foodie sympathizer group she could join. Where did clubs like that meet?

"Isn't that just a hoot? " Denise finished. It took Maureen a moment to realize she'd stopped talking. She panicked, not knowing what Denise had asked. She picked something benign.

"Yeah," Maureen said.

"Well, I think you're done. What do you think? Is that what you were imagining?"

Maureen swished her hair from side to side. She really did feel lighter and brighter. Denise's hairstylist magic had worked. Her hair looked better than ever. This was just what she needed.

After her haircut, Maureen found herself almost skipping down the street. She swished her hair and reveled in how much cooler she felt. She could almost imagine a breeze through the sticky air. Matthew still thought about her! It was such exciting news. She felt much less crazy for continuing to think about him. She wondered how to contact the

Foodie sympathizers. Maureen giggled to herself.

Besides Travis, another person she knew who might have information on prohibited activity was the man who owned the appliance repair shop. He also trafficked in black market goods. Maureen went to him to sell things when she needed cash quickly. She also liked to peruse his selection of books, although she hadn't had the money or the courage to buy one.

After work, she walked to the shop, past Sally's Bar and past the hair salon. She was careful to only walk under store canopies so she could remain in the shade. When she opened the door to the shop a little bell attached to the door rang and a man stepped from a doorway behind the counter. He wore the orange coveralls of a merchant. He had dark hair and a thick, bushy mustache, which Maureen thought was prohibited facial hair. He also wore little round wire rimmed glasses, which was also odd since Maureen assumed he probably had enough money for the corrective surgery. She wondered if maybe the glasses were an affectation.

"Why hello, what can I do for you today?"

Maureen glanced around the room, looking at vacuums, televisions and sewing machines sitting on shelves around the room. She was too scared to say why she'd really come so she said, "Can I see your latest shipment?"

"Of course, right this way."

The man lifted the curtain behind the counter and

he followed her through. They entered a room that looked like a disorganized library. It had floor to ceiling bookshelves piled high with books. Most of the shelves were two books deep with books placed sideways above them in every open space. Treasures Maureen couldn't identify were scattered across the floor. Large paintings were propped up against bookshelves. They maneuvered around some large pieces of intricately carved furniture. He led her to a particular shelf and said, "These are the latest. I haven't organized them yet. And those too." He pointed to a large pile on a roll top desk. "Are you actually going to buy one today?" he asked kindly and with a smile.

"Probably not," Maureen confessed. "But I love to look at them. I hope you don't mind. It's like a whole other world in here."

"I understand. You're not the only one who likes to look. And you do give me some business occasionally. That I appreciate."

Maureen picked up a heavy hardbound copy of *The Great Gatsby*. She held it in her hands. She lifted it to her face, opened the book and smelled the pages. It smelled like a forgotten paradise to her, a place she'd been but couldn't quite remember. She set it back on the desk.

"I was actually hoping you might have some information. I understand if you don't want to give it to me or if you don't have it and I don't want to be a bother..."

"Spit it out, girl," he said in the way that Maureen imagined a grandfather might say. Maureen paused, not sure how to continue.

"I'm searching for a friend of mine. We've lost touch. And you know how difficult that can be these days...finding friends." Maureen eyed the shopkeeper. He nodded, understanding.

"It is difficult to find friends. I'd like to think that you might find one in me," he responded. Maureen breathed a sigh of relief.

"Maybe you know my friend, Anthony Plumber."

The man glanced around the room like he was trying to see if anyone overheard. As far as Maureen knew they were the only people in the shop. Perhaps she was wrong. He looked her up and down, trying to assess her.

"This friend of yours is not always so friendly — to strangers. You've known him long?" Maureen's heart was beating in her ears. Was she making a huge mistake? She nodded. The man found a piece of paper and a fountain pen. He scribbled a quick note and thrust it into her hand.

"You'll find your friend here. Be careful." The bell rang, signaling someone had entered the shop. The shopkeeper startled at the sound. Maureen stared at him. She had been expecting a conversation.

"Go," the shopkeeper said, more emphatically. Maureen lifted the curtain and walked through to the front of the shop, glancing at the tall, thin man in black coveralls waiting at the counter who seemed to make the shopkeeper nervous. As she opened the door the shopkeeper called to her, "It'll be ready on Tuesday." Confused and a little worried, she opened the crumpled paper to read the message. It wasn't until she was outside that she realized it was pouring rain.

CHAPTER 6

Maureen leaned against the side of the building, staying under the overhang. She read the address. It wasn't far away. She heard a cracking sound and a yelp from inside the store. Maureen glanced at the curtained window behind her. She didn't dare interrupt a confrontation with someone in black Jasper security coveralls. She hesitated for just a moment and realized that her presence wouldn't help the situation. She felt like a dirty coward as she jogged off down the street towards the address scribbled on the paper.

She was soaked through when she reached what she hoped was Anthony Plumber's apartment. She rang the doorbell and looked down. She was dripping on the welcome mat. She reconsidered her timing and turned to leave when the door opened. A large, muscular bald man wearing brick red coveralls answered the door.

"Yes?" he growled.

Maureen was intimidated by his appearance. The

reality of what she'd heard at the shop and the potential danger she might be in slapped her in the face.

"I should go," she started.

"Nope," the large man grabbed her by the arm and dragged her inside the apartment. He slammed the door. "What are you doing here? Who sent you?" he bellowed.

"I, um, you know the man with the appliance repair shop?" Maureen found herself unconsciously backing away from Anthony. He walked towards her.

"Eli. Yes?"

"He gave me your address."

"Now why would he do that?"

"Because I asked for it?"

"Why?"

Maureen's retreat ended when she backed into the wall. Anthony continued slowly walking towards her.

"I heard you might know where Matthew Miller is." Anthony had reached the wall. He put one hand against the wall, beside her head.

"Now why would I tell you anything?"

"I, I don't know. I knew Matthew in school. He was my best friend and I wanted to find him."

"You're lying. Who sent you?"

"What? No, no I'm not!" Maureen shook her head emphatically. Anthony's other arm slammed against the wall beside Maureen's head. She flinched. She was trapped. Anthony leaned his face close to hers and spoke slowly and quietly.

"Tell me. Just say a name."

"No one. I mean, just Eli. I asked about you."

Anthony leaned back. "No. Eli doesn't give information that easily. There's no way. Tell me the truth. You have a minute." He glanced at his watch.

"Until what?"

"Until I kill you." He whispered it casually. Maureen believed the large man in her face.

"I, I don't know anything!" her voice shook. "I came to you for information!"

"And you expect me to believe that?" Anthony's right hand moved from the wall to her throat. "Just who do you think you are waltzing in here with this lame-ass story saying you just want information? No one is that naive." His hand started to squeeze.

"Maureen Baker," she whispered. Anthony's hand dropped and he stepped back.

"What? What did you say?"

Maureen bent at the waist and coughed. "I'm Maureen Baker, and yes, apparently I am that naive," she said looking at the floor.

"Maureen Baker? No way." Maureen glanced up. Anthony's back was to her. He seemed to be mumbling to himself. He turned back to her, studying her. "Maureen Baker? There's no fucking way."

"How do you know me?" Anthony ignored the question.

"How old are you?" he quizzed her.

"Twenty." Anthony appeared to be thinking.

"What are your parents' names?"

"Bill and Nicole Baker but they're dead." An expression Maureen couldn't identify crossed Anthony's face.

"There's no fucking way. Get out of here." Anthony held up his arm and pointed at the door. "Go away. I don't have time for this."

"Whatever you think I am I'd like to prove it to you. What do you want from me? How do you know me?"

Anthony paused again. "Tell me about Matt," he said finally.

"He was my best friend. He's tall. He has dark hair. He's really smart. He was the only person I ever felt...connected to, like we saw the world the same way. And now he's gone and I want to find him. I think you know where he is."

"Matt's a coward. He defected. But maybe if you're who you say you are, you can help me." He thought for a moment. "I can't believe that you're part of the movement and I haven't met you until now. Where have you been hiding? No wait. Don't tell me. It must be a safe house." Maureen didn't follow everything he was saying but moments earlier he'd been trying to strangle her so she kept silent.

Anthony turned his back to Maureen and started pacing around the room. Despite the fact that Anthony had threatened to kill her Maureen desperately wanted to trust him. She needed to trust someone with what she knew and what she didn't know. She hadn't quite made up her mind to trust Anthony yet but the words fell out of her mouth before she could think about it.

"Wait. I may be Maureen Baker but I'm new to all this."

"What does that mean?" Anthony stopped in his tracks.

"I'm not really a part of the...movement. Or maybe I am but I'm new."

"I don't follow."

"I just heard about Matthew and I started asking questions and it got me here."

"How is that possible?"

"I wanted to find Matthew and I'm curious about the Foodies but I don't know much. I was just trying to get some information. You know, you really need to work on your network. It was way too easy to find you..."

"Then — you don't know?"

"Don't know what?"

"You really don't know?"

"What are you talking about? You seem to know who I am. How is that possible?"

"That's not really important right now. I guess I should tell you what you're involved in. Sit." Anthony sat the kitchen table and pointed to a chair for Maureen. Maureen realized that a kitchen table was where families used to gather to share meals. Now it was where people met to conspire.

"I sympathize with the Foodie cause but I don't

think that abandoning everyone in Harvest to die is the answer."

"Die?" Maureen gasped.

"You really don't know a damned thing, do you?" Anthony shook his head and wiped his giant hand across his face. "Maybe you should just go. I feel like I just told you that Santa Claus isn't real." Maureen caught the allusion to the mythical figure that used to bring children presents the night before Christmas. She knew who Santa Claus was from books. No one celebrated Christmas anymore, of course. She perked up at the mention of esoteric knowledge. It was something that Maureen had a lot of and valued highly.

"It's OK. I never believed in Santa Claus. I don't believe in Jasper Industries either." That made Anthony smile.

"I'm working for positive change here. But obviously I'm failing since you've never heard of me and didn't know my group existed. Matt was on board for a while. Then he just gave up and defected."

"I can help," Maureen felt the need to cheer up Anthony. She didn't really know what he was talking about but she wanted him to be more hopeful.

"Maybe. We'd built so much and he just—sorry. I'm a little bitter. Most folks that work with me for a while give up and defect. Maybe that says something about me..."

"No. It sounds like what you're doing is really difficult. Not everyone can handle that. Apparently not even Matthew."

"It's hard but it's worth it. Maybe with you helping me I could—No, I'm not going do that. I'm not
going to use you—especially since...I can't. Maureen,
I would love the help. Lord knows I need it but I can't
ask that from you if you don't know what you're getting into."

Maureen was surprised by his antiquated use of
the word "Lord." She briefly wondered if he was a
believer, there were so few these days.

"You can teach me. You can tell me what I need
to know. I really want to help."

"It doesn't matter. You should go. It's getting
dark."

"Can we talk again? I have so many questions..."

"No. I'm sorry. It was good to meet you." Anthony raised his eyes from the table and smiled. "You're
shorter than I thought you'd be."

"What do you know about me?" Maureen's temper erupted. "How do you know who I am?"

"It doesn't matter now. You should go before it
gets dark and the patrols start."

"No! Tell me something!" Maureen stood and
then realized her mistake. She couldn't hurt Anthony
Plumber. He easily had a hundred pounds on her.
She had nothing to threaten him with.

"Maureen, don't do this. Just go home."

She was crushed. Anthony Plumber was supposed to enlighten her. He was supposed to have the
answers but now she just had more questions. Hot
tears stung her eyes. Maureen tried to hide them by

turning her head.

"You should go," Anthony encouraged gently.

Maureen obeyed. She didn't argue. Maureen desperately wanted to trust Anthony. He seemed sincere and it seemed like a difficult decision for him to tell Maureen she couldn't help him. He seemed to be protecting her from something but Maureen didn't know from what.

Outside she had to walk quickly. It was later than she'd thought. She walked so quickly she didn't have much time to reflect on the bizarre course of events before she arrived home.

When Maureen got to her apartment she stepped inside and sat on the chipped linoleum floor with her back to the wall. Had she always been this unhappy? Had the unhappiness only recently started to crush her or were the long-term effects finally showing? Maureen tried to hold onto the hope of her library card but it wasn't enough anymore.

One of the few people she'd ever felt connected to had left to join the Foodies. Maureen decided she didn't care if it was reckless or stupid she wanted to talk to Travis. Maybe Travis could tell her if the Foodies were dangerous or not. Maybe he could tell her where they were. Maybe she could visit. Maybe she didn't have to leave Sam after all. Maureen decided she'd talk to Bernadette in the morning.

She stood and instantly felt better. Talking to Travis seemed to be the answer. Everything seemed less pointless than it had a few minutes earlier.

Maureen couldn't remember what to call that emotion. What was it called when all felt lost and then suddenly you saw a great light? Oh yeah, hope.

CHAPTER 7

The next evening Maureen gave Bernadette a call and asked if she could come over. Bernadette was all too happy to oblige.

"Sweetie!" Bernadette cooed when she opened the door. She hugged Maureen tightly. "How are you?"

"I'm fine. I have a favor to ask." Bernadette ushered her into the apartment.

"Would you like anything to drink?" Bernadette asked.

"No, thanks. I was wondering if you could get me Travis Carpenter's phone number or address." Maureen sat on the pink couch and Bernadette sat on the opposite end.

"Whatever for?"

"My brother says he has a huge a crush on me. Turns out he's liked me for years but he's too shy to say anything. Sam said it would just kill him if I called him. He asked me not to but I can't pass up the opportunity. I've always liked Travis so I'd like to call him so we can go out," Maureen lied.

"Really? Travis Carpenter? He likes you and you like him?" Bernadette bounced on the couch in excitement. "Hmm well I must say that red hair has always been adorable but I didn't think he was your type."

"I don't want to miss a great opportunity."

"OK, I can do it. But it'll take a couple of days and it'll cost you. I know it seems like I'm rolling in dough but I don't have the money for that kind of bribe. This seems like an awfully expensive way to get a date."

"How much is it going to cost me?"

"Probably about thirty dollars."

"Thirty dollars! I don't have that kind of cash! How could a phone number cost that much?"

"Well, maybe you could just find a date the old-fashioned way. Why won't your brother give you his number? That seems really weird. Maybe there's a reason he doesn't want you to go out with him."

"No, no. I'll get you the money. I told you, Travis is embarrassed. He made Sam swear not to tell me. I'll get you the money in a couple days, OK? Thanks so much Bernadette." Maureen stood and headed for the door. "You can give a speech at our wedding."

Bernadette smiled broadly. "Oh, Sweetie! I would be honored!"

Back at her apartment Maureen surveyed the contents, trying to decide what to sell. She didn't have much of value and thirty dollars was a lot of money. She had a few pieces of jewelry that had belonged to her mother. She had some spoons in a kitchen drawer and a metal object shaped like a flower that someone had told her was a cake pan. She wasn't sure if those were worth anything. She had a new pair of work boots; those might sell. She had a poster of a Joan Miró painting on her wall. It was a rich saturated blue with black and red streaks. She wondered if that was worth anything. It was the only decoration on her walls. It was a gift from her father when she was a little girl, when those kinds of frivolous decorations were still available. She would miss the poster.

While she was scavenging through the apartment she pulled a slim, tattered spiral-bound book out from between the springs of her pullout bed. Maureen thought about the books she remembered as a child that were no longer available at the library. But this book was even more dangerous than most. This was the kind of book that, if found, could mean her disappearance. This was a family cookbook.

When Maureen's great-grandmother, Addy, had gone off to university her mother had made her a recipe book. It was filled with some of Addy's favorite recipes and recipes that she could easily prepare for herself. The pages were brittle and stained with what Maureen could only assume was food. The words on the page were foreign to her. One recipe was called Meme's Cornbread Dressing. Maureen knew that dresses had once been a style of clothing for women, like pants without legs. Why would you eat a dress? Maureen had trouble making sense of the ingredient list because she couldn't imagine the finished product.

Recipe books had been rounded up and put in libraries, just like other books but recipe books were seen as particularly subversive. If you had a recipe book, maybe you were cooking and if you were cooking maybe you were eating too. If you were eating, clearly you were hoarding resources. Maureen loved having the little recipe book. It made her feel dangerous. Addy had not given up the recipe book when the authorities were seizing them. Even though she was no longer able to acquire the necessary ingredients for the recipes she still saw some value in the little book. She hid it and treasured it. She passed it on to her daughter who passed it onto, Nicole, Maureen's mother. Nicole had given it to Maureen before she'd disappeared or died, depending on whose story you believed.

Maureen read the recipe for *Grandma Cake.*

1 c shortening

2 c sugar

¼ t salt

3 c plain flour

3 t baking powder

1 ½ t vanilla

1 c milk

4 eggs- one at time

Mix in order given and beat just until mixed good. Take 1 c of mix and put red cake color in it. Mix it on top of other mix. Mix just enough to make marble effect. Bake in greased tube pan. 375 degrees, 1 hr 10 min

The little recipe book was Maureen's favorite possession even though it read like a foreign language. She didn't know what the little letters next to the numbers meant. She couldn't identify some of the ingredients, even with all her food research. The cramped script handwriting was difficult to read. She liked to feel the pages of the book. She would read the recipes and close her eyes and try to imagine the smells, the tastes, what it looked like. It helped her feel connected to her dwindling family. She'd never met Addy but it helped her feel like she had. Maureen didn't know how to explain that to anyone. She hadn't even told Sam that she had the book. Her mother told her to keep it a secret. Maureen carefully wrapped the book in the white handkerchief and placed it back under the bedsprings. This was one thing she wasn't selling for Travis' phone number.

The next day, Maureen walked to the appliance repair shop after work with little sapphire earrings in her pocket. She opened the door and, as always, the shopkeeper, Eli, emerged from behind the curtain. He smiled at her.

"Have you come to smell the merchandise?" he asked.

Maureen was shocked to see that he had a black eye. His little round glasses were bent and sat askew on his broken nose. He had a large abrasion on his check. Maureen didn't know how to react. She had never actually seen the results of Jasper security agents before, only heard stories. Maureen wanted to comment on the state of his face but knew better.

"How was your friend?" Eli asked.

"Not as well as I'd hoped."

"That's often the case with that particular friend. I hope you have others." Maureen wondered at his meaning but knew they wouldn't be able to have a real conversation about Anthony in the shop.

"I have a proposition for you. I'm not sure if you'd be interested," she began, surprised at herself for being so cautious. The shopkeeper nodded, encouraging this line of conversation.

"I see you have an iron that needs to be repaired. Let me see it," he said. Maureen pulled the tiny sapphire flower earrings with a diamond center out of her pocket and placed them on the counter.

"The iron won't heat anymore. I'd hate to have to buy a new one," Maureen said.

"Ah, I see," Eli said picking up the earrings and examining them. "How *long* have you had this particular iron?"

"Um, maybe *thirty* years?" Maureen said, hoping she understood the question correctly.

"I think you're mistaken. This must be at least thirty-two years old." Eli placed the earrings under the counter and held out thirty-two dollars and passed them to Maureen. He winked at her.

"The iron should be ready on Thursday. Thursday," he said.

"Thursday," she repeated. "Thank you, sir."

"Eli," the shopkeeper said.

Maureen smiled. "Maureen," she said.

"I know," Eli whispered. "Thursday," he repeated loudly.

Maureen left the shop.

After she sold the earrings she went directly to Bernadette's apartment. She was afraid she might lose her resolve. Maureen had never held so much money before. Her hands shook as she handed it to Bernadette. Bernadette asked how she'd gotten the money. Maureen said it didn't matter. Bernadette said she'd have the information in a few days.

.

CHAPTER 8

Two days later Bernadette called Maureen with Travis's address and phone number. Maureen thanked her. Bernadette reminded Maureen to tell her how the date went. Maureen distractedly told her she would while she was trying to figure out how far away Travis lived.

In about ten minutes she'd walked to his apartment. She stood poised outside his door. She hesitated, wondering if she really wanted to get in deeper. She thought about the shopkeeper, Eli, wondering what happened to him and wondering what was going to happen on Thursday. She thought about Anthony Plumber and their initial confrontation. Maybe Travis wouldn't be friendly. It had been years since she'd seen him.

So much had changed in the past few days. Maureen had never heard a man being beaten before. She'd never been threatened, at least not outright. Anthony had threatened to kill her and she'd believed him. She'd survived the encounter and now she was a new person. The world she lived in now was different from the world she'd lived in a few days ago. There was no turning back. She wondered if Travis knew what the words in the cookbook meant. Maybe he could tell her and with that last thought she knocked on the door.

Travis answered after the first knock, as though he'd been standing right by the door waiting for someone to knock.

"Hello?" he said.

"Hi Travis. I'm Maureen Baker, Sam's sister. Remember? I was wondering if I could talk to you for a bit."

"Wow, Maureen? You look so different. Yeah, sure. Are you planning a surprise party for him or something?"

"Something like that. Can I come in?"

"Sure, sure, of course."

Travis opened the door wider and let Maureen inside. Travis was tall and gangly. He had fair, freckled skin and bright red hair. He wore burnt orange coveralls, which meant he was in transportation. Maureen remembered he worked for Jasper Industries but so did almost everyone else. She couldn't remember exactly what he transported.

"Please sit. Would you like some H_2O? I have colors." Travis ushered her inside.

"Yes, please. Do you have pink?" Maureen walked to the sagging couch and sat down.

Travis smiled. "Pink is my favorite, too."

Travis busied himself in the kitchen pouring the

H_2O into a glass and adding a couple drops of pink food coloring.

Maureen took a deep breath. "Travis, I'm not having a birthday party for Sam or anything. I don't want to lie to you. Please don't get mad at Sam. He asked me not to talk to you but I just can't help it. I asked Sam about Foodies since a friend of mine from high school became one and he said you...uh... know some things about them. I was wondering if you'd talk to me about them."

Travis handed Maureen the pink H_2O. He set his glass down on the coffee table as he sat down next to her on the couch. Travis had a way of staring at people like he could see into their souls. Maureen had always found it disconcerting and now was no exception.

"If Sam didn't want you to talk to me about this how did you find me?"

"I...I have some connections...I bribed an official."

"You bribed somebody?! How much did my address cost?" Travis seemed flattered.

"I don't really want to say. It was kind of a lot."

"What do you think I know that's worth all this?"

Travis didn't blink. He didn't glance away. He just kept staring into her soul. Did he know her true motives? Did he know what she really wanted to ask? Maureen was so rattled by his stare that she blurted out, "Have you really tasted food?" Travis laughed.

"Is that what this is about?" He glanced down, picked up his H_2O and took a sip. Maureen relaxed and sipped her own H_2O. Travis put the glass back down on the table. He folded his arms across his chest and sighed.

"Maureen Baker, if I hadn't known you since you were five I might think you were a Monitor." He laughed uncomfortably, continuing to make inappropriate eye contact. This time he really did seem to be searching her. He glanced around the room and then back to Maureen. He leaned down and whispered in her ear, "Where did you get the money for the bribe?" He kept his head low for her answer. She whispered back, "Eli." Travis nodded. She seemed to have passed some test. He narrowed his eyes a bit and then seemed to make a decision.

"Yeah, I've eaten. I don't even know how to begin to describe it to you. It's like nothing else. I've had cookies and pie. They gave me cheese once. I've also eaten green beans, just a few tastes of just a few things. It changes everything. You know, sometimes I wonder why I'm still here. I guess it's for my family. My mom would just die if I became a Foodie but sometimes I think about it—what it would be like."

That was exactly what Maureen had hoped for. She wondered if he'd told Sam these things. Maybe he could sense that she knew things, too. Maybe he'd never told anyone this before.

"What are they like? The Foodies? Are they crazy or are they like us? Where are they?" Maureen paused and then said what she'd really wanted to say, "Will you take me to them?"

Travis laughed. He seemed kinder and more sincere than Maureen had remembered, although she hadn't seen him much since he'd graduated high school. It probably wasn't fair to make all your judgments of someone when they were sixteen years old.

"How did they find you?" she asked.

"One day at work about a year ago, a man approached me as I was about to get into the truck to make a delivery. The man who approached me looked a little off. He was wearing old coveralls. It was color-coded in a way I couldn't identify. He didn't have an emblem on his nameplate and the pockets were closed with snaps instead of Velcro. I don't remember them ever being snaps. But the weirdest part was..."

"He was a Foodie!" Maureen exclaimed, interrupting him.

Travis sighed and took a sip of H_2O. "Yes, but the weirdest part was," Travis paused to see if Maureen would interrupt him again. Travis smiled ever so slightly knowing that he was torturing her. "The weirdest part was he knew my name," Travis finally finished. "I asked who he was and he asked for a ride. I only had a couple deliveries so I said OK. I should have been worried or suspicious but I was just curious. I don't tell many people this but I think you'll understand: I really hate my job. I know I'm no brain but I think I could do more than drive a truck, you know?"

Maureen nodded in understanding. She felt the

same way. Wasn't there more to life than being a preschool teacher or a hairstylist or a truck driver? Why couldn't they find what it was?

"I wasn't too worried about breaking protocol by taking a passenger. Hell, I break the rules all the time. He didn't say anything until we got further away from Jasper Industries. Then he said his name was Richard Fischer. He asked if I'd like to make some extra money. I said of course. Richard asked if I would be willing to make some delivers about once a month. I said sure. He thanked me, shook my hand and asked to be let out of the truck. We were on the side of the road between here and Allandale. I said sure, stopped the truck and he hopped out. I turned to say goodbye and he'd gone. I mean it was a flat field. I didn't see him walk away. He was just gone."

"That's it? And you weren't scared? You weren't worried it was something illegal? Did you suspect they were Foodies?"

"I wasn't scared. There was something reassuring about Richard, like I'd know him a long time, like an old family friend or something. I was positive whatever I would be transporting would be illegal. The coveralls showed he wasn't registered but I hadn't figured him for a Foodie. I just figured it was normal black market stuff."

"So then what?" Maureen prompted.

"Wait, what time is it?" Travis asked. The look on his face changed.

"It's almost eighteen hundred hours." Maureen glanced at her standard issue watch.

"I'm meeting my...mom. I've got to go. Come back tomorrow. We'll keep talking. It's good to be able to talk to someone. Around eighteen hundred hours." He ushered Maureen out the front door, locked it and ran past her down the stairs. Maureen was confused and a little concerned by his sudden departure but relieved that she felt she had someone to talk to.

CHAPTER 9

All day at work Maureen was distracted. She was focusing on coveralls. A few different styles were allowed but no one's looked like Richard Fischer's, the man Travis had described. She tried to think through the color codes in her head. At this point there were too many to memorize. She could only remember the big categories.

That night she went to Travis' apartment at eighteen hundred hours, like he'd said. She rang the doorbell. Travis answered immediately, just like he had the night before. He didn't look pleased to see her.

"Come in," he said as he pushed her through the door, looking over her head as if he were checking to see if she'd been followed. He closed the door behind her.

"Is everything OK? You seem nervous."

"I am, a little. Nothing to worry about, just the usual stuff."

"You always check to see if your guests have been followed?

Travis looked at her like he was trying to decide what to say. They made eye contact for what felt like hours to Maureen.

"Sit." Travis motioned toward the couch and Maureen sat.

"What's going on? Please tell me."

"I don't want you to get involved. I don't want to put you in danger. Sam would never forgive me if something happened..."

"What would happen? What's going on?"

"I—" Travis started then shut his mouth. "I can't. You probably shouldn't come here anymore. Maybe we can meet somewhere else. I'd love to talk to you about Foodies. We just can't do it here anymore."

Maureen stood and put her hand on Travis's shoulder, "Tell me what's going on."

Travis sighed. "I think I was followed last drop. I can't be sure but if I was followed then they know I'm helping Foodies. I could be in a lot of trouble. So I just—I don't want to put you in danger, OK?"

"Why weren't you nervous yesterday?"

"It might be nothing but a man bumped into me on the street earlier today. He was wearing Jasper Industries security black coveralls. He looked me right in the eye and said, 'Watch it. You need to be careful.' The way he said it, I just knew he didn't mean walking. It was something bigger. They have to know. I don't know if I can help anymore."

"Really? You'll have to stop? But what about the Foodies?"

Travis brushed off her hand and turned away from her. "Maureen, they might throw me in jail or they might make me disappear. I can't. It's not worth it." Travis glanced around his apartment. "I don't feel safe here. Can we go somewhere?"

"Sure. Sally's is just down the street."

Maureen worried about going out with Travis in his jittery state. He was going to attract a lot of attention. Maureen hoped people would guess they were on a first date. Travis checked all the locks three times before they left the apartment.

On the short walk to the bar Maureen grabbed Travis's hand and squeezed it tightly. She intended for it to be a reassuring gesture but Travis didn't let go of her hand so they walked to the bar silently hand in hand.

At the bar they found a quiet table in the corner. They both ordered Pinks. "Travis, if I'm making things worse we don't have to keep talking."

"No, it helps. I've wanted to talk about it but Sam wouldn't understand. There are things we don't talk about. He doesn't like it when I trash the CDT or when I complain about my job. Your brother's a great guy but he's kind of a Timmy."

"I know. He didn't used to be. I think after our parents died it was easier to accept his place in life. It helped him make sense of things. If he starts questioning the little things I think he thinks he'll question the big things too. I think that scares him. It's a lot easier to be a Timmy and just do what you're told without questioning it."

"All the Timmys I know seem so happy."

Maureen laughed. "I know! Why are we so diffi-cult?"

"I've actually wondered that. Is there something about us intrinsically that makes us unhappy? Would I be unhappy no matter what? Am I missing the gene that makes you content?"

"I wonder why everyone isn't unhappy. Do peo-ple live in a different world than I do? Am I the only one paying attention?"

"I know!" Travis slammed his palm on the table. "It's like if you knew what I knew you couldn't possi-bly be happy! Maybe we're the only ones who get it."

"Maybe." Maureen hadn't had a frank discussion like this in a long time. She didn't know that other people felt the way she did. Travis smiled at Maureen. His stare wasn't as intimidating as before. Travis took a sip of his H_2O.

Maureen shifted the conversation. "What are you going to do?"

Travis sighed. "I don't know. This didn't feel dan-gerous before. It was fun and exciting. But I think now I have to stop the deliveries. I'm really going to miss it. I feel bad; they're great folks. I wish I could keep helping them and I wish I could take you there. You'd love it. But I don't think this is worth my life."

"Right. How are you going to tell them?"

"I can send a message. There are channels. They'll understand." Travis's mind seemed to be wandering.

He took another sip of H_2O. "You know, maybe this *is* worth my life."

"Wait, what? What are you talking about?"

"I mean, what am I doing with it? Driving a truck for Jasper Industries? Whoo hoo! Big deal. Maybe this is more important than I am."

"Travis! Don't say that! You're so important. To Sam. To me."

"Am I really important to you?"

Maureen paused. That seemed like a loaded question and she wasn't sure how to answer it. She didn't want to lead him on but she didn't want him to sacrifice his life for a group of people he hardly knew.

"Yes, so important. You would be missed by a lot of people. You can't be thinking this way."

"But like we were saying, I'm so unhappy. Wouldn't I be better off fighting for a good cause?"

"Your life is worth living. Stop talking this way." Maureen grabbed his hand across the table. "You have to tell them you can't make any more deliveries. Promise me."

Travis stared at her. He didn't respond. He squeezed her hand. "Will you meet again tomorrow? Here about eighteen hundred hours?"

"Yes."

They parted ways, walking in opposite directions towards their apartments.

The next day at work Maureen couldn't stop thinking about Travis. She was worried about him. She was also worried that what he'd said made sense to her. She also felt like her life was meaningless. Maybe hitching her wagon to the Foodies would make it matter. Maybe she should talk to Anthony Plumber again. Her mind was so busy the crying children hardly registered all day.

After work Maureen arrived at Sally's bar a few minutes early. She hopped up on a stool and ordered a Pink. She took out her EZ Meal pellet and took Third Meal. She wasn't sure if they were planning on dining together. It seemed a lot to presume so she decided to eat before Travis showed.

Maureen drank her H_2O. She played with a fraying pocket on her coveralls. She pondered Thursday, trying to decide what might be happening at Eli's shop. Thirty minutes passed. Maureen tired of watching the nearly mute news on the TV behind the bar. She realized she didn't have Travis's phone number with her and decided to go to his apartment. Maybe he'd lost track of time. In the back of her mind she thought something might have happened to him but she pushed that thought aside.

She walked the few blocks to his apartment and walked up the stairs. Maureen rang the doorbell. No one answered. She waited and rang again. She knocked. Maybe he'd forgotten. Maybe she had the time wrong. Maureen waited a few minutes, rang the doorbell and knocked again.

She gave up and walked home. She wondered if she should be worried about Travis. She didn't know why he'd rushed off the other night but she was pretty sure if wasn't to meet his mom. Maybe his apartment was bugged or his truck. What if their entire conversation had been recorded? Would they come for her next? She hadn't done anything wrong!

Maureen thought about going to Sam's. She realized she'd have to tell him she'd been talking to Travis. If Travis were in danger Sam would miss him soon. Maureen went to her own apartment, taking a circuitous route, halfway worrying someone might be following her and halfway just wanting time to think. She found herself glancing over her shoulder and keeping an eye out for Jasper Industries security black coveralls. But anyone could be a Monitor. She was suddenly suspicious of everyone. When she arrived home she turned the news on the television. The turned the volume up, hoping it would drown out her worries.

The next day after work Maureen rushed over to Travis' apartment. She rang the doorbell, half expecting no one to answer ever again. Travis answered almost immediately, like he had that first day, as though he'd been waiting for her.

"Maureen. Come in." There was recognition in his voice but no warmth.

After the door closed behind her Maureen asked, "Travis, what happened last night? I was worried."

"What do you mean?" Travis looked confused.

"Weren't we supposed to meet last night?"

"Were we? I don't think so. I wasn't here. I had a

meeting. I wouldn't have scheduled anything on top of the um..."

"Meeting," Maureen finished.

"Right. The meeting."

Maureen quickly ran through the list of possible explanations for Travis' behavior. Travis was planning to run away with the Foodies and didn't want her to know or Travis had been caught, tortured and brainwashed. In Maureen's mind that was it; those were the only possible options. Maureen started to feel warm. Her heart was beating too fast.

"I—I think I have a meeting too. I almost forgot about it. Thanks for reminding me," Maureen said.

"Are you sure you have to go? Would you like some H_2O?"

Maureen had an idea. "Do you have any colors?"

"No. I think there's no need for them. What's the point of colored H_2O?"

"OK, well, um. I've got to go or I'll be late for the meeting."

"OK. Would you like to talk another day? Do you have my phone number?"

"I do. I'll call *you*. OK, bye Travis."

As he waved goodbye Maureen spotted what looked like ligature bruises on his wrists. Maureen ran down the stairs, catching her breath before she left the building. She knew that she couldn't run without wearing the proper jogging uniform. She realized she was going to have to tell Sam. Something was seriously wrong.

Back at her apartment, Maureen tried not to think about what could have happened to Travis. She was sad that he didn't remember any of their conversation from the other day. She already missed that Travis.

If someone got to Travis, did they know about her? Was someone searching for her now? Did they know she had been asking questions? Who scrubbed Travis? Maureen's head swam with questions and regrets. Maybe if she'd asked different questions she'd know more. Maybe they shouldn't have met at Travis's apartment. It was too late now.

He hadn't even told her anything about Foodies yet. All she had was the name of Travis's passenger, Richard Fischer. Yet again, Maureen cursed the general lack of public information. Maureen had heard that in some parts of the world people had access to the Internet. Maureen was convinced the government of Harvest was trying to keep information from them. She wondered what was out there.

Her thoughts returned to Richard Fischer. She needed to ask Anthony about Richard. Anthony seemed well-connected. Maureen was frustrated with him but he and Eli were now the only people who could give her information. She must have something that Anthony wanted. There must be a way to get him to talk to her. Now she wasn't just assailing her curiosity. She felt like she was trying to protect the people she knew. Maybe she'd be able to help Travis.

Maureen tried to come up with a way to keep an eye on Travis. In her hysteria Maureen didn't hear the knock on the door until it became a loud bang. She screamed. Then, shaking, she tip-toed to the door and peeked through the peephole.

It was Sam. Maureen let him in and closed the door. She whacked him on the arm. "Why were you banging on my door? Are you trying to scare me to death? What do you think you're doing?"

"Whoa there. Calm down. What's wrong? I thought you had the TV on loud or something." Sam took Maureen's chin in his hand and studied her face. "What's going on?" he asked with renewed concern. "Why are you so upset? Did someone die?"

"Maybe," Maureen mumbled, turning away.

"Wait, what? Maybe? Who *maybe* died?"

"OK, you can't get mad. Please don't be mad at me."

"Oh no, what did you do, Maureen? What did you do? Are you going to lose your traveling privileges?"

"This isn't about traveling privileges!" Maureen yelled. "What's so great about traveling privileges anyway? It's not like I get any vacation and the only place I could go would be Allandale. Ooh Allandale! I don't give a crap about traveling privileges!" A light went on in Maureen's brain. "Traveling privileges are meaningless! Totally meaningless! We don't get any time off and we're only allowed to go one village over if we ever do. But they use them as a threat! You'll lose your traveling privileges for doing this or that. But what are traveling privileges? They're nothing! It's an empty threat!" Maureen finished her rant, smiling like she had received a new spiritual teaching.

"What are you talking about? What happened? We don't have to talk about traveling privileges. Just tell me what's going on."

"Travis," was all Maureen could manage, getting her breath. "Something is wrong with Travis."

"How do you even know that? I told you not to talk to him."

"I'm sorry but just listen to me. Does Travis like colors in his H_2O?"

"Yeah, his favorite is pink. He always orders it when we go out. Why are you worried about him liking colors?"

"He doesn't like colors anymore. He said it's stupid. I think they've done something to him. They've changed him. He doesn't remember things. He had these bruises...I think someone tied him up." She gulped. "I think he was scrubbed."

"What are you talking about and what does this have to do with traveling privileges?"

"It doesn't have anything to do with traveling privileges! I think he's been found out. I think they know he was helping the Foodies and they've scrubbed him. He's not the same. You should go see him. See him and tell me he's not scrubbed."

"What did you talk about that is this important?"

"He gave me a name: Richard Fischer. He said Richard Fischer contacted him to make the supply runs. Richard Fischer knew Travis' name. He knew him. How did Richard Fischer know Travis? How can I find him?" Maureen left out the things that

Travis said he couldn't tell Sam. She wouldn't be the one to share those secrets.

"I know about Richard Fischer. I still don't understand. What are you involved in?" Sam held her by her upper arms. "What's going on?" he pleaded.

"I don't even know if I know. You need to go see Travis. Please. See if he's OK. I think—I think he's gone."

"I got all that but why?"

"Because of his Foodie involvement! Don't you understand? I think I've set something off..."

"What are you talking about? You asked Travis about the Foodies and now Jasper Industries is after him? You know that sounds insane, right?"

"I do. I know it sounds crazy but it's not just talking to Travis. I may have...talked to some other people too."

"Who? What have you been doing? I thought the Foodie thing was a passing interest."

"It may be a little more than that now..."

"Maureen, you've got to stop whatever you've been doing. It's too dangerous. Mom and Dad,"

"What about them?" Maureen yelled, interrupting.

"Mom and Dad got interested in Foodies too."

"You never told me that."

"I thought it would make you even more interested in them. I think it might have been what got them killed."

"I thought you believed the accident story!"

"I never said that. I just said I thought they were actually dead. There's a big difference. You thought that something was up because we never saw the bodies. I knew they'd died suspiciously. Look, what I'm trying to say is don't repeat Mom and Dad's mistakes. You can't go looking for this Richard guy. You just can't. It's too dangerous."

"I can't believe you never told me about Mom and Dad," Maureen whispered.

"I'm sorry. I didn't think you could handle it. Maureen, you have to tell me everything you know." Sam grasped her by the arms again and shook her gently. "You said you've been meeting with people. Who else have you been talking to? Besides this Richard Fischer, what do you know?"

Maureen had never lied to her brother before but something deep inside her made her say, "Nothing. No one. That's it."

"OK, I'm going to see Travis. I hope you're wrong about all this." Sam gave Maureen a quick hug and left.

Maureen sat on the floor with her head in her hands. She'd had no idea her parents had been involved with Foodies. Maybe after Sam calmed down she could ask him some more about it. Did they know Foodies? Were they just curious? It seemed odd for Jasper Industries EZ Meal scientists to be involved with Foodies. Maureen needed to know more.

Her thoughts turned to Travis. He might be changed, lost forever and it was all her fault. She hoped she was wrong and that everything would be all right. A part of Maureen knew that nothing would be all right ever again. Now she wouldn't be able to find Richard Fischer. It was much too dangerous. She would never get to see Matthew Miller. She would never get her questions answered. She would never eat. She sighed. In a way, even though she desperately wanted to see Matthew and she wanted to know more about the world, not eating felt like the biggest loss. It was a connection with her ancestors that she would never know.

CHAPTER 10

Sam didn't call Maureen the next day. She supposed he was too upset about Travis to talk to her. She understood he might need some time.

The moment she opened the door to her apartment, returning home from work, the phone rang. She answered.

"Maureen. It's Anthony. We need to talk. Sally's Bar in five." Maureen barely had time to agree before he hung up.

As she walked to the bar she remembered it was Thursday. Maybe Anthony would know the significance of Eli's message. Perhaps it was why he wanted to meet with her today.

Anthony was already seated at a table when Maureen arrived.

"You need to be more careful," Anthony said by way of greeting.

"What are you talking about?" Maureen asked, sitting.

"You can't see Travis Carpenter anymore."

"He's my brother's best friend. I've known him

forever. Why would anyone care?" Maureen's first reaction was to defend herself. She almost forgot what happened to him. Maureen lowered her gaze to the table. "I have to tell you something. I think Travis has been scrubbed."

Anthony slapped his hand on the table. "Shit! Not Travis! Damn it. That changes everything." Anthony paused; he seemed to be contemplating the next move.

"Eli told me something," Maureen started.

"Yeah," he responded absently.

"He told me to come back for my iron today. Does that mean anything to you?"

"He said what?" Anthony said, suddenly much more interested in what Maureen had to say.

"I...um...had a business transaction with him and he told me my iron would be ready on Thursday. He said it like three times. Thursday."

"We have to go," Anthony stood and pushed Maureen in front of him.

Out on the street Anthony started walking quickly to Eli's shop.

"What does that mean, about the iron? Is it a code?" Maureen asked. Anthony didn't look at her. His gaze was focused off in the distance. Maureen followed his gaze and saw a plume of black smoke. She started to run. Anthony held her back.

"Act curious but not too concerned. We can't run," he hissed in her ear. They walked quickly to Eli's shop. The entire shop was engulfed in flames. Firemen stood outside, hosing the neighboring buildings, attempting to keep the fire from spreading. No one emerged from the building. They stood close enough that the smoke stung Maureen's eyes. The air smelled heavily of kerosene. This was no accident.

"Do you think he's safe?" Maureen asked.

"Don't know."

"Did he start the fire? Was he trying to tell me..."

"Don't know. Oh, God. This is bad. Either way this is bad."

"The last time I saw him he'd been beaten up."

Anthony turned to look at her. "What day was that? Do you remember?"

"Monday, I think. Maybe Sunday? All those books...All those treasures..."

"That you never saw," Anthony said pointedly. "Meet me. Tonight. In about an hour. I've got to meet a friend. And I hate to do this but it has to be after curfew."

"What? I can't!"

"It's the only way. You won't have to travel in the dark. Come before curfew and stay until morning."

"I don't think I can."

"Maureen, you have to. Do it for Travis."

"Why can't I meet you now?"

"Travis. You saw what happened to Travis. I don't want that to happen to either of us. If it happened to you...I can't even imagine the consequences. Please. It's the only way. I have to talk to this friend."

"Where do you want me to go?"

Anthony gave her instructions. Maureen returned

to Sally's, sat at the bar and ordered a pink H_2O. She took Third Meal and stared mindlessly at the television. The television was muted. She watched the newscaster's lips move without paying attention to the closed captioning at the bottom of the screen. She thought the news made more sense this way. At least this way she didn't feel like yelling after watching it. She left the bar as soon as she could.

The air was still heavy with smoke as she followed Anthony's directions. They led her to the industrial side of town. She never had a reason to be there so she didn't know the area very well. The smokestacks billowing with black smoke, the smell of something burning, the grayness of this side of town was all new to her. It was deathly quiet. The streets were deserted. Anthony's directions were easy to follow. She quickly found the abandoned red brick building he had described. It had a faded painted sign on the side of the brick. Maureen tried to decipher it but couldn't. There appeared to be a picture of a baby in a wide bonnet. She went down into the basement. It was not at all what she was expecting.

There was a full kitchen like she'd never seen. She saw a sink and an oven with a range very similar to the one in her apartment. She turned a knob until she heard a popping sound. The burner lit. The gas was connected. Maureen's heart skipped a beat. She watched the low, blue flame dancing and smelled the excess gas. It took all her self-control to simply turn it off and walk away.

One wall was covered with floor to ceiling book-shelves. There was a beautiful oil painting of a nude woman on the wall. Next to it was a watercolor of a wooded landscape. It was like the shopkeeper's back room but it seemed more complete. That was a store. This seemed to be a home. Did Anthony live here?

Maureen admired the paintings. Art was strictly monitored and actually somewhat discouraged. Nudes were no longer allowed. Maureen had been taught that a painting of a nude woman was filth so she was surprised that she thought it was beautiful. She admired the soft lines of the woman's body, so like her own.

There was a wooden table with two benches in the middle of the room that appeared to have seen generations. Lit candles sat in the middle of the table on recently-polished silver candlesticks. Maureen sat, waiting for Anthony. As she sat she couldn't help doubting herself. What had happened to her? Why was she in a dark basement waiting for a man she hardly knew, a man who'd threatened to kill her once? Maureen was able to scold herself but she couldn't quite feel afraid.

Anthony Plumber arrived shortly after nightfall. He smiled at her warmly. "I'm so glad you came. I was worried you wouldn't." He sat at the table across from Maureen.

Maureen smiled back. "This place is wonderful. What it is?"

"It's my collection. I come here to remind myself

why I haven't left."

"Couldn't you just take all this stuff with you?"

"Maybe but it's not the same. If we take all the books, art, history, and food with us what does that leave people here?"

"But do you share this with people here?"

That seemed to sting Anthony. He glanced away. "I should probably tell you, I was born a Foodie."

Maureen gasped. "Oh my gosh! What's it like?"

"It was paradise." Anthony paused and smiled. "But I couldn't give up on everyone else. Nobody there cared what happened to the village, to the rest of the world. The things I know—I couldn't keep them to myself. I had to help. I left when I was a seventeen. I think people don't understand what I'm trying to do."

"What are you trying to do?"

"I'm trying to fix everything that Jasper Industries broke. I know you get it. You know that so many things are wrong with the way things are. You know that keeping books locked up is a tragedy, that art is more than beautiful, and that we're missing something more than food not eating together around a table."

Maureen did. She felt like she was talking to Matthew again. Anthony had just listed the things she couldn't put words to, the things that were missing. She remembered feeling an emptiness, even before her parents died. Life seemed to be all about following the rules and not getting in trouble. Everyone seemed to be just getting by, just trying to get through the day. Maureen felt certain that wasn't what life was supposed to be about. It seemed too tragic and awful. This room seemed to encompass what she thought it was missing.

"How do you fix all that?" Maureen asked, anxiously, wanting a simple answer and wanting it now. Anthony sighed heavily. He stared at the ceiling for a beat.

"Honestly? I don't know." Anthony looked at Maureen seriously. "You're probably in danger now. Being here. Talking to me. Maybe I should have told you that sooner."

Maureen shivered but she had known. Anthony had threatened to kill her. She knew she was in dangerous territory. It had been much easier for her to ignore her instincts than it was for her to ignore what Anthony was saying. Maureen shook her head.

"I don't understand. I just wanted to see Matthew. I pretended to be James Bond for a couple days and somehow now my life is in danger."

"Who's James Bond?"

Maureen sighed. "Nobody. I don't understand how it got this far. When I heard Matthew became a Foodie I realized how much I missed him. It also made me more curious about Foodies. Matthew and I were so much alike. Since he became a Foodie it made me wonder..."

"If you should join them too?"

"Maybe. We had the same questions and it

seemed like he'd found the answer."

"I can't tell you what to do but it would mean so much to the cause if you stayed. There aren't many of us left..."

"How many are there?"

"Well," Anthony paused for a long time, "Just us, I guess." He seemed embarrassed to admit that. Saying it out loud seemed to deflate him, all the energy left his face.

"Don't take this the wrong way."

"But?"

"But it doesn't really seem like you're *doing* anything. You have this great room full of forbidden stuff. You talk very passionately about fixing things. But what are you actually *doing*?"

Anthony was clearly upset. "I do a lot, OK? A lot. It's a really complicated thing. There are a lot of problems. And I'm trying to fix them all on my own! And I don't have any help."

"I understand," Maureen began, trying to smooth over his hurt feelings. "But I mean, what's the plan? How are you fixing things?"

"Well I haven't really had help until now..."

"Anthony, I don't care how many people you have. What is the plan of attack? How are you going to fix such a broad range of problems?"

"I don't know! OK? Is that what you want to hear? I don't know! I left to save everyone and I have nothing to show for it. I can't go back now. Listen, I don't need to hear 'I told you so' from everyone I've ever known." Anthony stood and starting pacing the room, mumbling to himself. Maureen watched, not knowing what to do. Anthony stopped in his tracks. "No. I'll just go back. This is useless. You're right. It's over." Anthony walked towards her. "You coming with me?"

He said it so casually Maureen almost missed it. Anthony had invited her to join the Foodies.

"Wait. What? A minute ago you were planning a revolution and now you're just giving up and going home?"

"Sure, why not? This is hopeless and it's been hopeless for a long time. You helped me see that."

"I didn't mean to shatter all your dreams. I was just looking for a concrete plan."

"And there wasn't one! There never has been. Are you coming?"

Maureen's head was spinning. "Where?"

"To the farm. I'm going home. Are you coming with me?"

"I, I can't. My brother is here. I can't leave him."

Anthony angered. "I thought you wanted to see Matt. Don't you want to eat? I thought you were on our side."

"I think I am. I do. But I can't go."

"Shit, if you knew...."

"Knew what? What am I missing?" Maureen yelled, emotion rising in her voice. Maureen stood and walked over to Anthony. She was sick and tired of not getting the full story. She punched Anthony in the chest as hard as she could. It felt like punching a brick wall. Anthony didn't react so Maureen punched him again.

"Tell me!" she said through clenched teeth as tears started streaming down her face. She punched him over and over until her hands ached. She fell to the ground at his feet. "Tell me how you know me! What don't I know? Are my parents alive?" Maureen wiped her face on her sleeve. She lowered her voice. "I never believed the lies from Jasper Industries. Do you know them? Do they miss me?" Maureen's voiced cracked and she started crying again. Anthony kneeled on the ground beside her. He held he wrists and stood her back up. He led her back to a bench and sat beside her. Maureen sniffled.

"I'm sorry I punched you."

"It didn't hurt." Anthony smiled.

Maureen did too. "I'm sorry I asked about my parents. That was crazy but it was the only idea that made any sense!"

"Because life doesn't make any sense," Anthony finished.

"Exactly! What am I doing?"

"What are any of us doing?" They sat in silence for a moment. Maureen was overwhelmed by how loud her breathing sounded inside her own head, like she couldn't fit another thought in her head, as though breathing was the only thing she could attempt in that moment.

"Come with me. To the farm. You belong there."

"I can't."

"Why? Because of your brother? That's a sorry excuse. He's living his life. You need to live yours."

"But I don't have anyone else."

"It's your life. If you want to live it for your brother that's fine but know that you had the choice to live it for you." Maureen shook her head. Anthony stood. He seemed to have used up all the tenderness he possessed.

"Fine. I'm leaving tomorrow. You're welcome to stay here tonight if you don't want to travel at night. There's a cot in the corner."

"Where are you going?"

"To my apartment."

"Aren't you afraid of traveling at night?"

"No. Why are you?"

"But the monitors!" Maureen called after him.

Anthony shrugged and walked out with an expression of sadness and defeat on his face. Maureen worried that she was the one who crushed his dreams. She couldn't believe that he'd invited her to join the Foodies. She hadn't known how to get in before and now she had a personal invitation and she turned it down for Sam. But it wasn't just for Sam. She was terrified. All the people associated with Foodies seemed crazy. It wasn't very reassuring.

She brought a candle from the table over near the cot. It seemed comfortable enough and was equipped with a blanket and a pillow. She carried a candle over to the bookcase. She skimmed the titles. She pulled a book off the shelf: *Casino Royale* by Ian Fleming. She flipped through the pages. It was in good condition. She put it back on the shelf. Anthony had it and hadn't read it. Maureen wondered how many of the books on the shelf Anthony hadn't read. Maybe that was his problem. She lay down on the cot and blew the candle out.

Maureen awoke with a start. She glanced around the room and quickly remembered where she was. She sighed loudly, remembering her conversation with Anthony. She wondered what would happen to all of his treasures when he returned to the Foodies. She reached for the candle and then remembered she hadn't brought the matches over. Maureen started to make her way across the windowless room with her arms outstretched. She knocked her shin on the wooden table in the middle of the room. She cursed loudly. She kicked the bottom step with her foot. Then she carefully climbed the stairs, kicking each step carefully with her foot. She reached the top of the stairs and turned the door handle. She let out a sigh of relief when it turned. The door opened into a room with windows. Finally Maureen could see the first light of morning. Technically curfew continued for another hour or so but Maureen decided to risk it. It was much easier to get out of morning curfew than evening. To be safe Maureen took back alleys all the way home.

CHAPTER 11

Maureen was lost in thought all day. Should she have jumped at the opportunity to join the Foodies? She'd thought she was so dangerous these past few days but when the opportunity was staring her right in the face she turned it down. She wasn't brave. In fact, even the dark frightened her. It was a common fear. They'd been programmed to be afraid of the dark but she'd felt like such a fool when Anthony left last night. Foodies probably weren't afraid of the dark.

Maureen tried to put a positive spin on everything. A decision had been made. She wasn't in limbo anymore. She was staying. Her home was here. Her family was here. That was that. She didn't need to run around playing detective anymore. It was over.

That night she called Bernadette and arranged to meet with her after work. Maureen decided that she needed to just act normal. She needed to let all this go.

"Sweetie! How did your secret date with Travis go?" Bernadette asked while hugging Maureen hello. Maureen cursed mentally. She had completely forgotten about that lie. She was juggling so many lies these days she couldn't keep track of them.

"It went all right. I don't think we'll go out again, though. I think we just want different things." Maureen tried to keep her answer as generic as possible.

"Oh, I'm so sorry! And after you paid all that money for his number you must feel like a silly goose now!"

"Yeah, something like that."

"Well I'm sorry it didn't go well. If you want I can give your number to my cousin, Herman...."

"No, no, that's OK," Maureen interrupted. How many times did she have to tell Bernadette that she wasn't interested in Cousin Herman? "I've been really busy. It's not a good time."

"Well, whatever floats your boat, Hon!"

The waitress came to their table to get their order. Bernadette asked for a little Gingko. Maureen asked if they still had colors. The rumors about the discontinuation were getting more insistent and Maureen felt she had to ask. The waitress said they had just run out. She offered Maureen some caffeine. She said she just wanted a plain. Maureen was more disappointed than she wanted to admit about the discontinuation of H_2O colors.

"Oh, I'm sorry. I know how much you liked those silly colors," Bernadette said. "This just isn't your day. Are you sure you don't want me to give your number to my cousin Herman? He's a real nice guy and I bet a date with him would cheer you right up!"

She wasn't going to drop this. Bernadette had been trying to get Maureen to go on a date with Cousin Herman for years. Maureen was confident that she wouldn't be interested in dating anyone that Bernadette set her up with. But it would make Bernadette happy and shut her up. Maureen did need something to do, a distraction. Maybe a bad date with Cousin Herman was just what she needed.

"OK, sure. Why not? You're always telling me how great he is."

"Really?! That's so great! I can't wait to tell him. He's interested in you too, you know. I keep telling him all about my great friend Maureen and he seems really interested in getting to know you. He'll be so excited!"

"Oh goody," Maureen lied through her teeth. "What did you tell him?"

"Well, just the other day, I told him how excited you were about Matthew Miller being a Foodie and how you were really interested in the Foodies. He seemed to find that very interesting. That was when he started asking for your number. Maybe all my stories about you have finally paid off. I've been saying for years what a great couple you two would make."

Maureen sensed that she might be interested in talking to Cousin Herman after all. Maybe he was interested in Foodies too. Maybe he knew something. Or someone. The waitress brought their H_2O and they had Third Meal. Bernadette had to excuse herself early. Her father was hosting a party and she was expected to make an appearance.

"I'll be sure to call Herman tomorrow! I'm so excited for y'all!"

"Me too." They hugged goodbye.

When Maureen got home she was surprised to see Sam standing at her door.

"Sorry. I should have called first. I didn't think you would be out."

"How long have you been standing here?"

"About an hour," Sam replied staring at his feet.

"An hour? And you didn't call me? Come inside."

Maureen ushered Sam into her apartment. He sat down at the kitchen table, the only place to sit in the apartment that wasn't Maureen's bed. She hadn't bothered to fold the couch back up when she got up that morning.

"Talk to me," was all Maureen said.

"I saw Travis and you're right. He's different. Something's wrong with him. The worst part is he doesn't seem to know. He doesn't know that something is different. There is a lot he doesn't remember, from before. He's not Travis anymore. I wonder what will happen when his family finds out." Sam stared across Maureen's apartment, not seeing. Maureen put her hand on his shoulder. It startled him and he jumped.

"I'm so sorry, Sam. I feel like it's all my fault. Travis was going to some meeting the day we talked. He left really suddenly and ran down the stairs.

Maybe what happened to him has something to do with that. It seemed really important and he seemed scared. Maybe if we can figure out where he went..."

"No! No, you're not doing any more investigating. This has gone far enough. I couldn't take losing you too. I just—I can't lose anyone else. I don't have much left." Sam stared at the floor, worrying a broken piece of linoleum tile with his foot.

"You're right. I'm dropping it. I'll stop playing Nancy Drew."

"Nancy who?"

Maureen remembered that, though she'd read them as a child, Nancy Drew mysteries were no longer available in the library. Sometimes Maureen worried that, because of the fictional characters that resided in her head, she lived in a completely different world from everyone else.

"Never mind." Maureen watched Sam's foot kick up little broken pieces of linoleum. "Sam, could you stop that?" He continued to break the linoleum. "Sam, please stop." He'd pulled up a whole square of the design. "Sam!" Sam looked up, startled again.

"What?" he asked as though he had no idea why she'd just yelled at him.

"Are you going to be OK?" Maureen put her hand on his arm again. He shrugged it off.

"I'm fine. I need to go home and take Cookie out anyway. I just wanted to let you know. And see you, see that you're OK. And you are. So I'll go."

Sam left abruptly.

The next day at work Maureen felt off kilter. All the kids were crying and she felt like she couldn't do anything right. Her co-worker, Elizabeth picked up a crying Amelia and asked, "Is everything all right? You seem distracted."

"I'm OK. I've just got a lot on my mind. Hey, do you like working here?"

"Like it? I'm very competent and I get compensated sufficiently."

"Right. OK."

"Here take Amelia. I've got to go break up a fight that's brewing."

Elizabeth thrust Amelia into Maureen's arms and ran off to break up a fight between two little girls. Amelia was still howling and Maureen had no idea why. Then she realized she didn't care why. Maureen wondered what would happen if she were no longer competent to work at the preschool. What would they do with her? Where would she go? That thought worried her enough that she started bouncing Amelia and cooing "It's OK. It's OK." Amelia calmed down and Maureen set her down. She realized that no matter what was going on in her private life she needed it to not show at work. She didn't need another reason for people to be watching her.

That evening she received a call from Cousin Herman. It was not at all what she had expected. Her apartment phone rang and she answered it.

"Hello?"

"Hello is this Maureen Baker? This is Bernadette's cousin, Herman."

"Oh hi!"

"I was wondering if you might like to take a walk tonight, before curfew, of course. We still have a few hours of daylight. I feel like we'll have a lot to talk about."

"I agree," Maureen answered, following his lead by not saying any details over the phone. Was he purposefully trying to meet outside so no one could listen in on their conversation? Maureen felt like a spy. She started to get excited but then had to remind herself how her latest escapades had gone.

"A walk sounds nice. Did Bernadette tell you where I live?"

"Yes, she did."

"Meet me in ten minutes?"

"Sure. See you then."

"Bye." Maureen hung up. She glanced at her reflection in the mirror. She pulled her heavy curly brown hair into a ponytail. She brushed off the front of her yellow coveralls. She briefly wished that her assigned color were more flattering. Then she wondered why she was primping for a spy meeting. She went downstairs to meet Herman.

Herman arrived right on time. He was much more handsome than Maureen had anticipated. With a name like Herman she hadn't had high expectations. She was secretly glad she had fixed her hair. Herman was built like a rugby player, muscular and compact. He wore dark blue coveralls and had sandy blonde hair.

"Maureen. It's so good to finally meet you. Bernadette has told me so much about you."

"It's good to finally meet you too, Herman."

"Let's walk," as he said that Herman wrapped her arm around his. It was a romantic gesture but Maureen wondered if it was so they could talk more quietly.

"I hear we have some common interests," he continued. "Bernadette told me that an old high school friend of yours became a Foodie. She said you are interested in them. Is this true?"

"Yes. I can't imagine that everything we hear on the news about them is true. They're just people with a different way of life. I'm curious about them."

"I think you're more than curious. Does the name Richard Fischer mean anything to you?"

Suddenly Maureen worried that Herman wasn't a friend. What did he want to know about Richard Fischer? She wished that she had a secret spy code word to use. Was Cousin Herman a Foodie friend or Foodie foe? Maureen decided that either way lying seemed safer. It was nearly the truth.

"No, I can't say that I know anyone named Richard Fish."

"Fischer. Richard Fischer."

"Ooh Fischer. Nope. I don't know anyone by that name."

"Are you sure?"

"I am." Maureen realized this wasn't really a lie at all, which helped keep her tells at bay. She had never met Richard Fischer. He was nothing more than a character in a story that Travis had told her. Travis. She felt so guilty for what happened to him.

Herman looked Maureen squarely in the eyes, like he was trying to figure her out. Maybe he was also wondering if she was a Foodie friend or Foodie foe. He glanced away. It seemed he had decided something.

"Maybe you're not the person I thought you were. Sorry for the mistake." Herman started to walk away.

"Wait! What are you talking about? Who did you think I was?"

He turned back to her. "I'm sorry. That was rude. I thought you understood that this wasn't exactly a social call. I apologize. I must not have made myself clear. I thought we had similar interests. I must have been mistaken."

Maureen racked her brain for a way to ask his opinion about Foodies without giving too much away.

"What do you think about colors for H_2O? Did you know they've been discontinued?"

"I did hear that," Herman said hesitantly. Maybe he sensed that this was a test. "I was sorry for it. I'll miss getting a Green after a long day at work."

Maureen breathed a sigh of relief. "I was a fan of Pink. I think maybe we got off on the wrong foot." She paused, wondering if this was the right thing to do. "I haven't *met* Richard Fischer but I have heard of him."

A broad smile spread across Herman's face. "I know that was hard for you so I'll go first."

Just as Maureen was letting out a sigh of relief, convinced that she'd done the right thing, a large black sedan drove slowly by them. Cars were uncommon. They belonged to high-ranking officials or Jasper security. Herman eyed the car with what Maureen could only call fear. He grabbed her arm again and pushed her into an alley, walking briskly. They quickly got to the end of the alley.

As they started down the sidewalk another black sedan drove up next to them. Maureen had noticed the first one's license plate started with an "M". This was a different car. The only time she'd seem this many cars on the road was during the parades for Jasper Day, the day they celebrated Dr. James Jasper, the savior of humanity. They walked briskly, turning down another alley. Herman pushed her up against the wall by some large trashcans in the alley.

"Why are they following you?" he spit out.

"I thought they were following you," she responded.

"What have you done?"

"Nothing," Maureen lied.

"What do you know?"

"I don't know what you're talking about. I just wanted to know more about my friend."

"You're lying," Herman said. They heard car doors slam shut.

"Let's go," he said, pulling her by the arm. They

continued down the alley and then out onto another sidewalk and then down another alley. They continued to zigzag this way down the street, trying to avoid the black sedans. Maureen counted at least one other car. Her heart was pounding out of her chest. She didn't understand what Herman had been asking her. Did he know whom she'd been talking to? That she'd been to Anthony Plumber's hideout? That she had known Eli? What did he know? What could she tell him?

Finally Herman broke a padlock on a door in an alley and pushed Maureen through it. It was pitch black inside. Maureen had a moment of panic. She wondered why she'd trusted Herman and then realized she didn't. They were being followed and they'd run together. He hadn't earned her trust yet. Maureen tripped over a box and started to fall forward. Herman caught her by the shoulders.

"Herman, I don't think," she started. Herman gripped her shoulders tightly, silencing her. Once again, they heard a car door slam. They heard the sounds of people walking. Maureen thought she heard a dog. Did they have dogs chasing them? What was going on? She heard the dog bark and some people yelling. The sounds died down, as though they had passed. Eventually they heard the car doors slam again and heard them drive away.

"What the hell?" was all that Maureen could think to say. "What the hell was that?"

"Jasper security. I'm surprised you haven't met

them before. You must be in pretty deep."

"No way! I haven't had a tail until I started hanging out with you! What's your story?"

"There's no time for this tonight," Herman said.

"Then when?" Maureen asked surprised at how rude she was being.

"Hey, look. I wanted to help you. I don't have to if you don't want it. I thought you wanted to see Matt." Maureen softened when she heard Matthew's name.

"I do. Give me a reason to trust you." Maureen was surprised by her straightforward question but they didn't have a lot of time. She needed to know he was an ally.

"I know Richard Fischer. I know that idiot Anthony Plumber," Herman began.

"Hey! Anthony's not an idiot! A little misguided maybe..." Maureen cut in.

"So you've met him," Herman replied. Maureen couldn't believe she'd volunteered that information. She needed to be more careful. "I know that Eli died in that fire earlier this week." Herman paused, letting that information sink in.

"Do you mean the fire at the appliance repair shop? Was that the shopkeeper's name?" Maureen tried to feign ignorance.

"You know who I'm talking about. All the books are gone." Maureen's face fell at the mention of the treasures that were lost. "I know you know a lot. I want to help you."

"I don't think I need your help," Maureen replied.

She didn't like Herman's attitude.

"You don't need my help? Jasper security almost caught you tonight."

"Caught me doing what?"

"It doesn't matter! They could arrest you for looking at them funny. You're on a list now, Maureen Baker." Maureen knew he was right. It didn't matter what crime she was charged with or whether she was charged with anything at all. If she was on a list, she needed as many friends as she could get.

"Look, I'll tell you more later. I promise. You can trust me," Herman said. They made their way through the maze of boxes toward the door. "I'll call you." Herman opened the door into the alley.

Maureen started to say something but she realized Herman was gone. It reminded her of Travis's story about Richard Fischer just disappearing. She looked up and down the alley but didn't see a trace of him. A strange thought occurred to her and she looked up at the sky. After glancing around for a few more moments she walked around a couple blocks before she headed home. She had to walk quickly since the sun was setting but it still felt safer than to go directly home.

CHAPTER 12

The next morning Maureen awoke, still dressed in her coveralls from the night before. She had fallen asleep on top of the blankets. She glanced at the clock and ran out of the door. How did she fall asleep so fast? Why hadn't she set an alarm?

She arrived at the preschool a mere ten minutes late. A few minutes after she arrived she excused herself. She ran to the bathroom to see how horrible she looked and to take First Meal. She swallowed her pill and re-did her ponytail and smoothed her coveralls. And then she breathed. What had happened last night? Who was chasing them? Was it really Jasper security? The biggest question was: could she trust Herman? She didn't have time to think about any of that. Elizabeth banged on the door. "Maureen? Are you in there? Where have you been? I need you out here!" As Maureen walked out of the bathroom Elizabeth handed her a crying child she didn't even recognize. Was this child new? Had she been so preoccupied lately that she didn't even notice?

Maureen barely had a moment to breathe all day

let alone think. She was meeting Bernadette at the bar like they always did on Tuesdays. Since Bernadette was always late she'd have some time to herself. She really needed some time to think.

After work Maureen dragged herself to the bar. She wasn't looking forward to seeing Bernadette. She just wanted to be home alone to work things out. Why did she think that if someone enjoyed colored H_2O they were friends of Foodies? What a terrible code! That didn't tell her anything! She had given too much away and the authorities would come and get her any minute. What a fool she had been!

Maureen glanced at her watch. Bernadette was later than usual. Maureen flagged a waitress down and ordered a plain. She might even take Third Meal without Bernadette. Where was she? The couple at the next table was having a loud conversation that Maureen couldn't help but overhear. The man had a prominent nose and nervously chewed on his lip when he spoke.

"I heard that James Jasper is working on a new product that's really going to revolutionize nutrition," he said.

"I heard that too. It's supposed to be coming out soon. They say it's going to replace colors for H_2O. I can't wait to see what it is," the woman with short curly blonde hair replied.

Normally Maureen was not one to interrupt strangers' conversations but she couldn't help herself. She turned to the man and the woman next to her.

"You mean Jim Jasper, James Jasper the third."

"Yeah, right. Dr. James Jasper," the man said, chewing on his lip.

"Dr. James Jasper died a long time ago. His grandson, Jim, James Jasper the third," Maureen articulated the name and relation slowly, as though speaking to preschoolers about not biting one another, "is the one in charge of Jasper Industries these days. He's also got a son named James Jasper. He's the fourth."

"Are you sure?" the woman asked, scrunching up her face in confusion. "I was pretty sure it was James Jasper."

"They're all named James Jasper!" Maureen exclaimed throwing her arms in the air. She took a deep breath. "They all have the same name but they're not the same person. The James Jasper who invented EZ Meal has been dead for years."

"Are you sure? He was testing EZ meal on himself for years before it was released to the public. I've also heard his house has a higher concentration of oxygen. It's helped to keep him young," the man said, chewing his lip.

"With all of Jasper Industries' innovations people are living much longer than they used to," the woman added.

The news constantly reported Dr. James Jasper sightings. Maureen figured there was no way the man was still alive but it further fueled the mystique of the company. She clearly remembered hearing about his death in history class in school but some people make such an impact on the world that people just won't accept that they died. It also further fueled the confusion that everyone was named James Jasper.

"How old is the oldest person you know?" Maureen asked, trying a different tactic.

"Wait what?" the man asked.

"How old is the oldest person you know?" she tried again.

"Um, I don't know. Maybe sixty?" he answered.

"Right. Sixty. Sixty is a long way from, I don't know, a hundred and twenty? What were you saying about EZ meal prolonging people's lives? They've actually published studies that say it lowers life expectancy but they don't know why. It's been widely reported. We're living shorter lives than people did when we ate." The woman gasped as though mentioning eating wasn't polite. The man frowned at Maureen.

"Well, I haven't seen those reports..." he said.

"They're everywhere. They've known it for years." Maureen turned away. This was a lost cause. She'd tried to have this conversation before but no one seemed to listen. They just regurgitated what the news told them. Where are all the old people? There weren't any. If EZ Meal was prolonging peoples' lives shouldn't there be a large population of older people? Maybe the Dr. James Jasper sightings helped distract people from that fact. Dr. James Jasper was a hundred and twenty years old! It kept people striving to be a hundred and twenty even though the oldest person they knew was sixty. Even though the cold hard facts were out there and they were available, people still refused to believe them. Maureen shook her head.

Maureen opened a breast pocket on her yellow coveralls and removed the EZ Meal pellet. She stared at it for a moment, rolling it between her fingers. Were these little pellets killing people before they reached retirement? Was this a mistake? She put the pill back in her pocket. Where was Bernadette? She took her phone out of her pocket. No missed calls. This wasn't like her.

She lazily glanced up at the television in the corner of the room and saw Bernadette's picture. It was a family portrait of Bernadette, her parents and her brothers, taken years ago. Bernadette looked so young.

"Freddy, can you turn up the volume?" Maureen asked the bartender. He dutifully turned it up.

"...Rogers family left town early this morning. Brooks Rogers, town magistrate, left a statement with his secretary saying that the family was going on a much-needed vacation and would be back in a few weeks."

Something was wrong. No one went on vacation because no one received any time off work. Going on vacation had become a euphemism for running away from something—or someone. Where could they have gone? Did they take Herman? Maybe this was all because of Herman. Traveling privileges only allowed travel to Allandale but as a town magistrate Brooks Rogers would be able to get further but how much further? Did the family have a car?

Maureen felt people staring at her. She met Bernadette at Sally's all the time. Why didn't she know her friend was going on vacation? Why was she there alone? She left a few cents on the table to pay for the H_2O and left. She walked as fast as she could to her apartment.

Once she was safely inside she called Herman. Part of her wished that he had gone with them so that he was safe. The other part of her wished that he were still in town so he could help her and explain what was happening. She felt like everything was crumbling around her and that it was somehow her fault. Every time she talked to someone, something bad happened.

As she listened to Herman's phone ringing she almost hung up. Maybe she should stop now. Sam told her to drop it. She didn't and now Bernadette was gone. And that might be all her fault too. Her finger hovered above the button to end the call, five rings and still no answer. Herman must be dead.

Maureen started to cry. How was she so alone? She suddenly felt a rush of warm thoughts about Bernadette. She spent so much time being annoyed with her. She didn't appreciate her enough. Her best friend was gone. She had destroyed Sam's friend, Travis. Sam was upset with her. Her parents were gone. Even Anthony Plumber was gone. She would never be able to find Richard Fischer and now Herman was probably dead too. If he wasn't dead, he was sending the authorities to her house right now. Maybe she would be dead soon, too. Maureen began to sob, her body shuddering with every gasp for breath. Everything was broken.

She looked down at the linoleum tile her brother had torn up. Maureen picked at the edge of the tile with her fingers and ripped a large piece up. It made a popping sound as the ancient glue gave way. She threw the floppy tile across the kitchen and screamed. It made a satisfying smacking sound when it hit the wall. Maureen ripped up another tile. She threw it across the room, her screams and the smacking sound blending together. After several minutes she surveyed the damage; almost half the kitchen floor was torn up. Maureen stopped ripping, thinking that she might need to destroy the rest of it sometime soon but decided that was enough for now. She ran her hand over the exposed glue, thinking how uncomfortable it would be to walk on it barefoot.

Maureen's phone rang and she let out a little scream. She crawled to the table, picked up the receiver to answer it and noticed her hand was shaking. She didn't say anything but let out a loud breath into the receiver. "Get out of your apartment. Now. Meet me at Jasper Park as soon as you can. By the playground. Now." Maureen wasn't in a mood to argue with an anonymous voice over the telephone. What did that say about her state of mind? She was about eighty-five percent sure that it was Herman. What about the fifteen percent chance that it wasn't him? What was wrong with her? Maureen stood up and examined her apartment. The floor looked awful. She suddenly felt guilty for destroying it. She had a strong feeling that this might be the last time she ever stood there. She wiped her face on the sleeve of her coveralls. She took the cookbook, wrapped in a handkerchief out from under her mattress. She took the last of her mother's jewelry out of her sock drawer and grabbed the last of her money and stuffed them in her pockets. She zipped the cookbook into her coveralls and left as quickly as she could.

Maureen practically ran down the stairs, almost running into her neighbor, Mr. Foley, on his way up the stairs with a large paper sack that was blocking his view. She didn't even apologize to him. She just ran. Jasper Park was a few blocks away.

Once she was out on the street Maureen wanted to keep running. Something inside her told her to run as far and as fast as she could. She needed to get away. If she ran down the street not dressed in the proper exercise uniform, however, she would arise suspicion. Someone might stop her just because it was unusual. No one wanted to appear unusual. It took all she had for Maureen to walk instead of run. She walked as quickly as possible.

A couple blocks down, Maureen saw a black sedan with tinted windows coming down the street very slowly. Maureen ducked down the nearest alley and walked a couple blocks on the other side before taking another alley right before the park. Maureen realized she'd done that without thinking at all. She'd done it on instinct. What had happened to her? Now she was suspicious of all cars. Life had changed so much in the past week.

When she arrived at the park, Maureen made her way to the playground, staying on the edge, near the trees. She saw a man doing the same beside the deserted playground. Maureen realized that there were no other people out. It wasn't past curfew. Usually the sidewalk was crowded with joggers, dog walkers and people pushing strollers at this time of day. What did they know that she didn't?

Maureen's stomach was churning. Alarm bells started to go off in her head. This wasn't the right choice. Go home! Go home! He's going to kill you! But Maureen didn't listen to the alarm bells. This was so out of character. Maureen realized that she had no context for any of this. She had no idea who to trust. Herman was one of the only other people she knew anymore. She remembered that most of the people she trusted were gone.

She walked right up alongside the man in the trees. She was a few feet away before she was positive that it was Herman. He grabbed her arm and pulled her further into the trees. "Go," Herman breathed into her ear. There was no one around them, which made Maureen wonder why he was whispering but he obviously knew more than she did. Herman moved quickly but quietly through the trees on the edge of the park, dragging Maureen along behind him.

Maureen felt like she was losing something she would never get back. She felt like she might never see Harvest again. She worried she might never see Sam. That thought made her sad but she'd realized in the past few days that this was much bigger than her little family. There were so many others involved. Maybe she could help make things right. At this point, following Herman through the trees, she had no idea what making it right would mean but she desperately wanted to know.

Herman led her out of the trees and into a large open field that she recognized as the edge of the village. Maureen panicked. There was no cover! Anyone could see them. She didn't know that the park could take you all the way out here. In her mind the edge of the village was so far away but here they were, in a matter of minutes. Maybe it was her world that was so small.

"Where are we going?" Maureen asked. Either Herman ignored her or didn't hear. They walked across the open field, thigh high with grass. Grass this high was unbelievable. The landscaping in town was immaculate and if it wasn't, people were punished. Maureen was worried of what might be hiding in the grass. Could there be snakes? Why was this grass so high?

"Are we going to Allandale?" Maureen used the name of the only other village she knew. Herman stopped dead in his tracks. He turned to Maureen.

"You don't know?"

"Know what?"

"There is no Allandale."

"What do you mean?"

"Have you been to Allandale? Do you know anyone who has?"

"I've never left Harvest," she responded with shame. "I've never been anywhere. But their sports teams are better than ours. And you can see the coast from there."

"None of it's real. I'm so sorry, Maureen. I thought you knew more. This is going to be harder than I thought. Maybe I shouldn't have — No, I had to. They were coming for you. I'm sorry. We have to keep going. We're close." Herman smiled what he must have thought was a reassuring smile. It seemed more like a grimace and worried Maureen even more. He must be even more frightened than she was.

Herman was holding Maureen's hand instead of her arm now. Maureen felt like Herman was holding her hand crossing the street. She wondered if he was holding her hand so she didn't wander off. Where would she go? She had no idea where they were. The grass here was yellow and dry, unlike the lush green grass in the center of town. Their legs swished through the tall, dry grass. It sounded deafening to Maureen. There seemed to be nothing here. Maureen couldn't see any buildings in any direction. The sun was starting to set. Maureen wondered if she couldn't see very far because of the darkness or maybe they really were that far away from everything, farther than she'd ever been.

Herman had lied about being close. Maureen thought she couldn't walk any farther. Through the humid air a warm breeze rushed across the open field. Maureen turned her face to the breeze, letting it wash over her. They never had this kind of breeze in the village. They'd been walking for hours, long enough that her eyes were adjusted to the dark. It was a full moon. Maureen thought the stars were leading their way. Her stomach rumbled. She remembered that she hadn't taken Third Meal.

"I haven't taken Third Meal. Can we stop a second so I can?"

"No."

"No we can't stop or no I can't take Third Meal?"

"Both."

"But I'm hungry," Maureen whined.

She opened the breast pocket with her EZ Meal pellet. She brought it towards her mouth and Herman hit her hand, scattering the EZ Meal pellet into the high grass.

"Why did you do that? I needed that!"

"No you didn't. We have to keep going."

"No! I'm not going anywhere until you tell me where we're going and why you just did that!"

"We don't have time for this. They might be coming

for us."

"We haven't seen another human being for hours. Please."

"They're killing you, the EZ Meal pellets. Don't take them anymore."

"What do you expect me to do? Starve to death?" Maureen reacted to her own hunger and frustration instead of the fact that EZ Meal was killing her.

"I expect you to eat," Herman pulled a small packet wrapped in wax paper out one of his cargo pockets.

"I was hoping to introduce you to better food first but this will have to do."

He opened the packet to reveal a hunk of crusty white French bread.

"Is that...bread?" Herman smiled as though he was finally convinced that Maureen was who he thought she was.

"Yes. Sorry I don't have anything to put on it, a fool eats bread with bread, but it will have to do. Take it."

Maureen was too distracted by the new object to ask about the strange proverb. She accepted the wax paper with the large piece of bread. She smelled it. It smelled like home, which was odd since her home had never smelled of bread. She'd never even seen bread before but it smelled familiar. She took a bite. It felt strange to chew. Maureen tried to swallow a large bite without chewing and coughed it up.

"Slowly. Chew it up before you swallow it. I

know it feels strange. How does it taste?"

"I don't know how to describe it. It's soft and chewy but crispy on the outside. I love the way it feels on my tongue. I don't know how to talk about it. It's wonderful."

A warm feeling welled up inside Maureen. How could anyone give this up? How could people take EZ Meal and not fight for this? She understood about The Collapse but why did they admit defeat? After two bites of bread Maureen was ready to fight for food.

"Herman, I..."

"Eat some more. We have to keep going. We're almost there." Herman pointed to a building off on the horizon.

Maureen hadn't seen a building for hours. She wanted to know what time it was but her watch didn't have a light on it since no one was allowed out after dark. She stared at the dial for a while but couldn't make out the time. Finally they approached the building. It didn't look anything like the pastel-painted brick apartment buildings in the village. It was made of sheet metal and much smaller than any building she'd ever seen. There was a combination lock on the heavy metal door. Herman knew the combination and quickly opened the lock. He opened the door and motioned for Maureen to go in first.

It was pitch black and Maureen couldn't see a thing. Herman picked up something near the door. He cranked a handle and light came out of the flashlight. There wasn't much to the room. There was a bed, a sink with a pump, and a wood-burning stove. Above the sink were shelves filled with rows and rows of cans and glass jars.

"Bathroom's out back. Sorry about that."

"What is this place?"

"It's a safe house. We should get some sleep. I can sleep on the floor..."

"No. Don't worry about it. We'll both sleep in the bed." Maureen surprised herself but she was feeling generous after eating the bread. They both removed their heavy black work boots. Maureen rubbed her feet. She poked at a few large blisters on the balls of her feet. They both got in bed and pulled the covers up to their chins. Herman fell asleep almost immediately. Maureen started to run through the day's events. Exhaustion quickly got the best of her and she fell asleep.

CHAPTER 13

Maureen awoke in a sweat. She didn't know where she was. She saw an arm that wasn't hers and realized she was in bed with someone. It was a hairy arm, a man's arm. She twisted around until she could see Herman's face. She let out a sigh of relief.

Yesterday's events came flooding back to her. They were in a cabin in the middle of nowhere. Herman had called it a safe house. She wasn't sure where they were headed or what the plan was. Were they going to meet Foodies? Maureen had no idea. The more she thought about it, the crazier it seemed. She didn't know Herman well at all but she believed everything he told her. He told her that Allandale didn't exist. He'd also told her that EZ Meal was killing her and he'd given her food. Maureen had eaten. That was what she'd wanted, wasn't it? Now if she could see Matthew all of her dreams would come true. Maureen felt that she had lost sight of what the point of everything was.

She wasn't sure if she should believe everything that Herman told her but some of it did start to make sense. Maureen was so exhausted that she didn't budge. She felt safe in the bed under the handmade quilt. She traced the bumpy quilting with her finger, imaging the person who'd made the quilt. She hadn't felt safe in a week. No, that wasn't true. She hadn't felt safe for years. Since her parents died she'd been afraid of losing again. At this very moment there were so many things to be afraid of and yet Maureen felt that Herman would help her through them. Herman would keep her safe. She felt sure of it.

Maureen closed her eyes and tried to fall back asleep. She couldn't push Herman's breathing out of her head. She started to hear birds chirping. Although Maureen would have been content to stay put she just had to pee. As she was trying to maneuver around Herman without waking him her stomach growled so loudly that it woke him.

It took Herman a moment to remember where he was too. He smiled shyly at Maureen. "Good morning," he said.

"Good morning," Maureen responded. "I was just about to use the restroom."

"Yes, of course." Herman swung his legs to the edge of the bed so Maureen could get out. She put her feet in her untied boots. Then she walked out back, like Herman had told her.

When she returned Herman was starting a fire in the stove. Maureen watched as he put wood in the firebox and lit it. He grabbed a pan and poured water into it from a jug. He opened a glass jar. "I thought I'd fix us breakfast. Again, I apologize that this is your introduction to food. I promise it's much better than this."

Maureen watched, hypnotized by Herman's actions. This was a show she had never seen before. Herman waited for the fire to get hot. The smell of the wood-burning stove was cozy but the little building quickly got stuffy. Herman opened the front door. Then he put the pot of water on the stove. When the water was boiling he added the contents of the jar. Maureen watched little brown circles falling into the pot. Herman picked up a small bag from the shelf and opened it. He smelled it and smiled. "Dried apples. This will help."

The small, shriveled dried apples didn't look like Maureen's mental image of the big, round red apple. Maureen searched her mental list of food. She pointed to the pot on the stove, "Oatmeal?" she asked, uncertain of her guess.

Herman grinned. "Yes. I'm making tea too. I was lucky to find some. I think you'll like it. I even found a small amount of sugar. You'll probably want to add that since you've never had it before."

Herman poured water into two metal mugs covered in chipped blue enamel. He dipped small strainers with leaves in the mugs. When the oatmeal was ready he spooned that into two metal bowls. He put some dried apples in the oatmeal and stirred. He passed a bowl to Maureen. Then he removed the strainers from the mugs and added some sugar to one and passed it to Maureen. All of these motions were foreign to Maureen. She'd never seen anyone prepare food before. She watched, enraptured. Herman's movements seemed so natural, graceful. It looked like a dance. Maybe he did this all the time.

Maureen accepted the bowl and the mug. She stared at them. Steam rose from both. The smells were overpowering and exotic. Maureen didn't know what to do.

"Oh sorry! I forgot to give you a spoon," Herman's magic words ended the spell. Maureen glanced up and took the bent spoon he handed her. He saw the panic in her face. She was completely overwhelmed.

"Here. You eat it like this," Herman raised a spoonful of oatmeal to his mouth. The spoon entered his mouth and then he removed the empty spoon. He chewed exaggeratedly and swallowed.

Maureen raised a spoonful of oatmeal to her mouth and thrust it in. She immediately spit it back into the bowl. "It's hot!" she exclaimed.

Herman tried not to laugh. "Sorry. I forgot to warn you. Let it cool for a moment."

When she could stand it no longer Maureen tried another bite and then another and another. She shoveled and shoveled until it was gone. The new experience was over too soon. She looked at the empty bowl with a touch of sadness.

"We'll have lunch, too."

"Second Meal," Maureen said.

Herman smiled like a pleased teacher. "You know

a lot for someone from Harvest."

"I read a lot," she responded, sipping her tea. "Oh, this is lovely. I could eat this all day."

Herman smiled at her misuse of the word but didn't correct her. After a few sips of tea Maureen remembered herself.

"What are we doing here? What happens next?"

"I was hoping to get through breakfast," Herman laid down his oatmeal bowl and picked up his mug. He closed his eyes and inhaled a deep breath, letting the smell fill him. He sipped the tea and let it sit in his mouth for a second before swallowing. Maureen watched and wondered if that was the customary way to drink tea. Was she doing it wrong?

"We're waiting for Richard. He's going to come and bring us to the farm."

"I get to meet Richard Fischer?!" Maureen let that sink in before asking, "Why did we have to leave?"

"They were coming for you. They've been tightening security and you'd been seen with me. You had to leave."

"How did you know?" Maureen asked, suddenly suspicious. Herman blinked once before responding.

"I have connections." He took another slow sip of tea. "I got uncle Brooks to leave town. It was hard to convince him but I feel better knowing they're safe."

"*You* told them to leave?"

"Yeah, the security team was onto me and I didn't want my family getting involved."

"Where did they go?"

"I don't know and I don't want to know. They went somewhere safe. That's all I need."

"Is Richard going to bring us to bring us to the farm?"

"I think so. Richard sent me a message telling me to come here and bring you. I'm not even sure how he knew about you — what you were involved in, that maybe you were in danger — but he's Richard Fischer. He seems to know everything. And everyone. I thought you were still pretty below the radar. You said you've never met him?"

"Never. I'd just heard about him from Travis."

"Travis...that was a big loss for us," he said shaking his head. "The Foodies in sectors eight through twelve relied on him. It might be weeks before sector nine gets....Oh never mind. You wouldn't understand anyway."

"Explain it to me. Please. I understand if you want to blame what happened to Travis on me."

"Why would I blame you? You didn't do anything."

"He was scrubbed days after he told me about Richard. I thought it might have been something I did. Could somebody have been watching me?"

"Why would anyone be watching you? You're just a preschool teacher — I mean, you're not important. Wait. I mean..."

"I got it, Herman."

"I didn't mean it that way. I meant- — what did you do?" It was the same question he'd asked her in the alley. Maureen didn't know how to answer it. She wasn't sure she fully understood what she'd done. Maureen studied Herman's face. He was still waiting for an answer. She shrugged. "You have got to be kidding me! I can't believe I got stuck babysitting you."

Maureen couldn't figure Herman out. He seemed angry at her lack of knowledge but he seemed hesitant to tell her things. She almost missed Anthony's secret knowledge about her. They sat in silence for a moment.

"So what do we do while we wait for Richard? Should we be doing something to um, help the uprising?" Maureen asked. Herman smiled, relaxing.

"No. We should just wait here. I can't wait to get back to the farm. It's been years since I was there. I wonder if Margie is still there..."

"Who's Margie?" Maureen asked, realizing as soon as she'd asked that Herman was somewhere far away.

"Hmm?" Herman asked.

"Can you show me all the food here?"

"It's not time to eat again."

"I know. I had plenty to eat. I just want to see it, to learn about it."

"OK, I guess."

One by one Herman took down the glass jars and earthenware containers filled with food and showed them to Maureen. She was able to correctly guess many of the items she saw. Her food knowledge impressed Herman and he asked her over and over again if she'd eaten before. She tried to explain her obsession and her food notes to him. Herman didn't seem to understand. Maureen even used the phrase "food historian" in trying to explain what she'd been doing. Herman wrinkled his forehead and narrowed his eyes. Maybe he couldn't understand her obsession with trying to unlock the secrets of foods past because he ate habitually. Food wasn't a thing of the past to him. It was simply part of his life.

Later in the afternoon they had some more tea and Herman fixed some lentils and rice for lunch. Maureen also ate that too quickly.

Finally around dusk, when Herman was starting to think about cooking dinner, they heard a knock on the door. Herman froze. He put his finger to his lips. Maureen felt the hairs on her arms stand up. She had been so sure the next person they would see would be Richard Fischer. Now she was frightened that someone else had found them. Maybe the smoke from the stove had attracted someone. Were people searching for her? Would anyone besides Sam be missing her? Did Sam even know she was gone?

Herman tiptoed to the door and waited. Someone knocked on the door three times: long, short, short. Herman slowly opened the door. It was only then that Maureen realized Herman had a long knife in his left hand, hidden behind his back. For a split second, Maureen wondered if Herman was on the right side, on her side. When Herman saw the man in the doorway a broad smile spread across his face. He ushered the man in and gave him a bear hug. Maureen saw a machete in the other man's hands. They had both been armed. Maureen wasn't comfortable until they both set their weapons down.

"Maureen, this is Richard Fischer. Richard, this is Maureen Baker."

Richard Fischer was older than Maureen had expected. He was a tall, handsome man with salt and pepper hair. He was wearing out-of-date tan coveralls. His face crinkled with smile lines as he smiled at Maureen.

"Maureen, I would have recognized you anywhere." Richard hugged her in a familiar way that made Maureen uncomfortable. Richard wasn't her uncle. He was the leader of sectors eight through twelve. How did he know her?

"I don't mean to be rude but have we met before?"

Richard completely ignored her question.

"I've got some bad news," Richard began, speaking to Herman. "You can't come back to sector eight yet. We have a mission for you. I need you to go back and get Travis Carpenter. We can't leave him there—like that. After what he's done for us, he's one of us now."

"Richard, we can't go back there. We'll get caught. And I'm sorry for what happened to Travis but there's nothing we can do for him now." Herman spoke with an even tone but he was visibly upset.

"That may not be entirely true. We're working on a new therapy. He could benefit from it. We can't leave him behind."

"It's too dangerous. Maureen almost died," Herman replied, his voice rising.

"I what? Oh no, Anthony wasn't really going to kill me." Richard and Herman stared at Maureen for a moment. She could see the question on both of their faces but instead they let it pass. Had she been in more danger than she thought? Then she had another thought: was Herman lying to Richard?

"I understand the circumstances but as your leader I order you to return and retrieve Travis. I hate that I have to send Maureen with you but you can't go alone."

Every word out of Richard's mouth flew over Maureen. How did he know her? Who was he? What was he talking about?

"Is what happened to Travis my fault? Is that why I have to go?" Maureen interrupted. Richard turned to her. His face softened.

"Of course not, Lamb. It wasn't your fault but Herman might need help getting him out of there. They might have surveillance on him. I think you can do this, do you?"

"Yes," Maureen answered completely honestly. She wasn't sure why he called her lamb but she was already sure she would do anything Richard Fischer asked of her. She couldn't understand why Herman was so reluctant. This didn't sound difficult.

"Richard. You don't know what it's like here. You haven't been there in so long. It's dangerous. Plus Margie..." Herman tried again. Richard interrupted him.

"I see now why she left you. You're a coward."

Richard looked directly into Herman's eyes. His voice was like ice. Maureen was glad he hadn't spoken to her that way. It was terrifying. Herman turned away from them and raked his hand across the stove, knocking three heavy cast iron pots off. He let out a growl. The pots clattered to the dirt floor. Maureen jumped. Herman stood with his back to them for a moment, breathing heavily.

"Will you do it or not?" Richard asked simply, staring at Herman's back. Herman turned to face him.

"I will," Herman responded.

"Good boy," Richard said. He turned to Maureen. "Take good care of Herman for me. I want both of you to come back here safe. OK, Lamb? We owe Travis this much, Herman." Richard put an arm around Maureen's shoulders and squeezed. He walked out of the small shack. Maureen walked after him, straining her eyes in the darkness, searching for him. There was no sign of him. The mysterious, powerful man was gone.

Maureen glanced back at Herman. He sat on the edge of the bed staring at the ground for what felt like an eternity. Maureen was afraid to speak. Finally he said, "I'm not hungry. Is it OK if we just go to bed?"

"Of course. Are we going back for Travis tomorrow?"

"Tomorrow night." They sat in silence for a beat.

"How does Richard know me?"

"I can't tell you. Let's just go to sleep."

"OK."

Maureen lay under the covers, staring at the ceiling, hoping that Herman's slow even breathing could put her to sleep. It was only then that she realized when he'd said he couldn't tell her how Richard knew her it could mean that he didn't know or that he knew and he couldn't tell her. Maureen sleepily decided to ask for clarification in the morning.

.

CHAPTER 14

The next morning Herman made oatmeal again and once again he apologized for feeding her oatmeal. Maureen could have eaten anything and been completely thrilled. Over breakfast they started working out a plan. Maureen thought they could just go to Travis's apartment and ask him to go with them. Herman assured her that was too simple. He said Travis was probably being watched and Travis might not know who either of them was. They might have to take him by force.

"But Travis knew me. He knew me even after he'd forgotten other things. We've known each other since we were kids. He's my brother's best friend. He knows me. He'll come with us. We don't have to kidnap him," Maureen protested.

"It's not going to be that easy. We can't just waltz into his apartment and expect him to come with us. Even if it did work that way, we'd be followed and probably caught."

"What happens if we get caught?"

"It depends. They might just scrub our memories;

we'd be left like Travis. And we wouldn't have some-body come back to get us unless Richard thought it was necessary," Herman said matter-of-factly. Maureen wondered why Richard deemed it "neces-sary" to retrieve Travis.

"Well, what happens if they don't scrub our memories? Would they kill us?"

"Probably not. We're not that important. If they caught Richard they'd kill him. If they caught the people who blew up that building they'd kill them. They shouldn't kill us — unless they decided to blame us for the bombing. But maybe dying would be better than losing everything you've ever known."

"But Travis didn't lose everything. He still knew who I was. Maybe Richard's therapy works. Travis is still in there."

"I'd love to believe you but I know more about this than you do. It's not possible that Travis remem-bered you. And Richard is great at manipulating people. He might have told us he has a new therapy because he knew it would make you cooperate. Rich-ard does what he has to."

"You don't believe him? Why don't you trust him?"

"I know that Richard does what he has to, to get things done."

"What did he ever do to you?" Maureen asked in frustration. Herman lowered his head.

"It's not what he did to me it's what he did to...I don't want to talk about it." He raised his head and spoke more confidently, "I have my reasons to distrust him. But I also realize that we have to do exactly what he says."

"Or else what?"

"Or else we go back to Harvest and pretend that everything is normal. We just keep sucking down our EZ Meals and try to forget that it's killing us. I can't go back there. Can you?"

Maureen shook her head.

"There's also the possibility that our memories will be scrubbed just for going back. We're trapped. We have to do what Richard says," Herman finished.

"But I want to do what Richard asked us. I think we should get Travis."

"Maybe that's why Richard wanted you with me. He knew you'd want to go. Maybe that's why he pretended he knew you."

"I don't think he pretended. I think he does."

"Do you know him?"

"No, but he said he'd recognize me anywhere. Maybe he met me when I was a child."

"Maureen, Richard lies. You really think he knows you? And that Lamb business. Seriously? You bought that?"

"Yeah, I guess I did." She paused, "Isn't a lamb a baby sheep?"

Herman let out an angry sigh. "Yes."

"Why would he call me that?"

"Why indeed? To manipulate you," Herman said, throwing his hands up in the air.

"How is it manipulating me if I didn't even understand it?"

"He knew I'd tell you it was a pet name. You have to listen to me if this is going to work. I hate feeling responsible for you. I don't want you to mess anything up and get hurt..."

Maureen cut Herman off, "You don't need to feel responsible for me. Let's get back to the plan. We'll need to get moving soon."

Maureen and Herman spent the rest of the day working on their plan. They ate canned fish and crackers for lunch. Once again, Herman apologized for feeding her uninteresting food. Maureen loved it. Anything new was exciting to her. She was still thrilled to be eating any food at all. Herman assured her that they would eat much better once they got to the farm on sector eight. During lunch Herman described the farm, the buildings, the fields, and the animals. Herman talked about who lived there. He talked about how excited he was to get back there. Maureen decided that they had to succeed in their mission, not just for Travis but also for Herman, who deserved to go back to sector eight. Maureen wasn't sure why he ever left it in the first place. Then she thought Richard probably made him leave. It seemed that Richard could make anyone do anything.

At dusk, Maureen and Herman left the cabin. They each had a backpack with rope, duct tape, and things they found in the cabin that could be used as weapons. They also carried water bottles and small stashes of food. Maureen didn't think that she could actually attack anyone with a knife but she didn't want to argue with Herman. She didn't really want to talk to Herman at that point. She wondered how he got involved in all of this. Maybe he'd followed Margie out to sector eight.

The trip back into the village seemed much shorter than that first walk out there. Maureen realized just how close to the village they really were. She wondered why Herman was so nervous. It seemed like it wasn't going to be difficult to get Travis.

"Please let me try to talk to Travis first. I promise if it doesn't work you can come help. I just want to try. That's all," Maureen had said back at the cabin.

"It's too dangerous. I wouldn't want," Herman paused, searching for a word, "anything to happen to you. We have to do it my way."

"And what's your way? We jump on him and bind him with duct tape?"

"You make it sound so inelegant."

"Come on. Give me, I don't know, five minutes. If I'm not down with Travis you can come in and save the day," Maureen said.

"He's not going to know who you are."

"He knew me. He'll know me again."

"That was days ago. He's losing memories. They'll be gone."

"Please just let me try. Five minutes."

"Five minutes?"

"Just five."

"OK. Fine. But only five minutes. After that I'm coming in guns blazing."

"We don't have any guns," Maureen said laughing. Herman didn't return her laughter.

∽

They stood on the edge of Jasper Park in the shadows, among the trees. It was just a few hours past curfew but it felt like the middle of the night. No one was out. They barely heard a cricket. Maureen tried to make the darkness feel peaceful but no mental gymnastics could make it feel anything but menacing. The heaviness and stillness of the air weighed on her.

They watched Travis's apartment building. It was one block over from the park. Only a few windows were lighted. Maureen had spent so much time in back alleys for the past few days that she had figured out a back way to Travis's apartment. They crept in the shadows until they arrived at the back of Travis's building.

"In and out, OK? If you're not out in five, I'm coming in after you," Herman said.

"OK, got it," Maureen said.

"If anything happens..."

"It's going to be fine. I'll see you in three minutes," Maureen said, trying to convince herself.

As she crept towards the back door she thought she heard Herman whisper, "I'm sorry." She glanced back at him. He waved her forward. Maureen shook off the thought that she'd heard Herman say something. After a lifetime of being taught to be afraid of the dark, the darkness played tricks on her.

Maureen slid through the door and tiptoed up the stairs. She stood outside of Travis's apartment door for a moment. She lifted her arm to knock on the door and saw that her hand was shaking. She let out a shallow, shaky breath. Her heart was pounding in her ears. Her palms were sweaty. She knocked on the door quietly. She briefly wondered if she would answer a knock on her door after dark, then she realized she no longer had a door. She didn't have a place to live. That thought caused a sense of panic to rise from the pit of her stomach. What the hell was she doing? For a moment she almost ran down the stairs and went to Sam's apartment. She didn't know Herman. She didn't know herself. She attempted to clear her mind of all doubt but only managed to relegate the doubt to a dull hum in the background.

She tried the door handle. It was unlocked. She slipped inside and closed the door silently behind her. "Travis? Are you home? It's me, Maureen Baker, Sam's sister. I know it's late but this is really important," Maureen said, just above a whisper. She heard sounds coming from the bedroom. She realized someone might have beaten her to Travis. She edged up to the door to the bedroom. She peeked inside and saw Travis getting undressed. She quickly turned back towards the living room. Maureen debated the best way to do this without scaring Travis to death. She decided there wasn't a good way to do this.

Herman would be there in minutes if she didn't get on with it.

Maureen stepped from behind the door once Travis had on a pair of regulation grey sleep shorts and a matching grey T-shirt.

"Travis, hi," Maureen said. Travis yelped and instinctively retreated from the voice. "Travis, it's OK. It's me, Maureen, Sam's sister." Travis continued to back away towards the bathroom. "Travis, tell me you know who I am."

Travis peered at Maureen with terror in his eyes. "I, I don't know you. What are you doing here? It's past curfew." Herman had been right. Maureen wondered what she should do for the next minute or so until Herman got there. She couldn't overpower Travis by herself. He was over a foot taller than her.

"I'm going to call and report you for breaking and entering. And being out past curfew. And for spying on me while I changed clothes. And..." Travis shrieked, backing away from Maureen as if she were a hungry lion.

"Travis! You've known me since we were kids. Sam Baker is your best friend."

"I don't know anyone named Sam. I just moved here. I hardly know anyone."

Maureen glanced around the room and noticed the boxes for the first time. The shelves in the living room were empty. Travis's clothes and shoes were in disorganized piles on top of boxes. Had he really left? Was this an elaborate plot by Jasper security? What had they done to him?

"I just need you to come with me. I don't want to hurt you. You're in danger."

"I'm not going anywhere with you. You can't hurt me."

Travis eventually backed himself into the bathroom and slammed the door behind him. Now Herman had a door to break down. Had it been five minutes? Where was he?

Maureen heard boots coming up the stairs outside the apartment door. At first she felt relief that help was on the way but it sounded like more than one person. That couldn't be good news. Maureen banged on the bathroom door.

"Travis Andrew Carpenter! Come out of there right now or we're both going to die here tonight!" She sounded convincing because she was sure that what she was saying was true. No matter who was coming up the stairs more than one set of boots spelled trouble. Travis opened the door a crack.

"Cookie? Do you know Cookie?" He had a confused expression on his face.

"Yes! Cookie is Sam's dog! You love Cookie!"

Travis slowly emerged from the bathroom just in time for his front door to be kicked in. It was unlocked! Maureen thought, angrily. She grabbed Travis's hand and started running for the fire escape off the living room window. Six men in black coveralls intercepted them. They wore ski masks and carried enormous guns. Guns were rare and these could only belong to Jasper security.

The men had her and Travis facedown on the floor in a matter of seconds. They secured their hands behind their backs with zip ties. They were gagged and bags were thrown over their heads. Maureen had a difficult time standing up. Two men pulled her up by her arms. As they did, one said quietly, "Let's go, Lamb." Maureen knew instantly that the voice was Herman's. She wished she had taken his apology seriously.

Maureen and Travis were dragged down the stairs and put into two waiting large black utility vehicles. Maureen had never been in a car before but she felt the movement once they began to drive. On the drive, Maureen wondered if Herman had always been an enemy. She also worried that she couldn't trust Richard Fischer. Maybe he'd set her up. Or Bernadette. She had to know that her cousin worked for Jasper security. But how was he also involved with Foodies? Had the shopkeeper Eli really died in that fire? Who started the fire and why? What did Anthony Plumber really know? Was he part of the set up too? What were they going to do to Travis? What had he done to get his memory scrubbed in the first place? Why would they bother abducting him after he had no memory? Were they going to kill him? What were they going to do to her?

Maureen started to hyperventilate. One of the men heard her distressed breathing and pulled the bag off her head and removed the gag.

"What the hell are you doing, McCoy?" a man riding in front called back.

"She was hyperventilating," McCoy responded.

"So she passes out. It's not a big deal," the man in front responded. "Put the bag back on." McCoy gently placed the bag back on her head.

"Slow deep breaths. Sometimes counting helps," McCoy said.

"McCoy!" the man in front yelled. Maureen heard McCoy move farther away from her. She took slow deep breaths like McCoy had suggested. She slowly counted to three. Breathe in. One, two, three. Breathe out. One, two, three.

McCoy was right, counting helped. Her current situation felt inevitable. She was sure she'd be caught eventually. She was almost relieved that it had happened; now she didn't have to worry about it anymore. Maureen spent the rest of the trip hoping that her memory would be scrubbed and she would be set free. Then she remembered Sam. Would she know him when she returned? Breathe in. One, two, three. Breathe out.

CHAPTER 15

Maureen awoke on a cot in what appeared to be a cell. It was about six feet by eight feet. The cell was three brick walls and one filled with iron bars. She looked out and catty corner to her own cell she saw Travis in a similar cell. He was still lying down. She wondered if they'd been drugged. She tried to peek down the hall. She guessed there were eight cells. There was a metal door at the end of the small hallway. No one seemed to be guarding them. In each corner of the hallway, by the door she saw cameras. It was deathly quiet.

Maureen glanced around her own cell. There was a small stainless steel toilet in the corner. She also saw a plate of food and a glass of H_2O. The beans and rice looked similar to the lentils and rice Herman had prepared the day before. At least, Maureen thought it was the day before. She had no way of knowing how long she'd been down there. She kept thinking "down" because there were no windows and she just assumed that all dungeons were underground.

She eyed the food suspiciously. She wanted to refuse it but she was too hungry not to eat it. She worried that it might be poisoned or, more likely, drugged. She decided to take the chance. Why would they put her in a cell just to kill her? She ate the entire plate of food. It was actually much more flavorful than the lentils that Herman cooked in the cabin. It burned the inside of Maureen's mouth a little but it was pleasurable. She ran through a mental list of food adjectives, not sure which one to apply. She decided it was the best food she'd eaten yet and in prison of all places.

She sat close to the bars and watched Travis. He appeared to be fine. If she sat very still she could see his chest rise and fall with his breath. She couldn't hear any movement. Her only hope of escaping would be when they were moving her. She briefly wondered if the process of erasing her memory had already begun.

In a way, assuming they were going to scrub her memory was comforting. It was the best-case scenario. She held onto that idea with white knuckles. Maureen tried to decide how erasing her memory would negatively impact her. She despondently decided it wouldn't change her life that much. Maybe she would be happier. She wouldn't remember Matthew, her parents or Bernadette, all those people who were no longer in her life. Part of her longed to be emptied to have the painful memories extracted from her mind.

Maureen awoke on the cot in her cell. She didn't

remember falling asleep. She couldn't decide if the food was drugged or if being in this cell made her narcoleptic. Without any way to tell the passage of time and nothing to do but think exhaustion overtook her. She lay on her cot and stared at the ceiling. She saw a small air vent. Without having to try, Maureen knew her hips would never fit through it.

She got off her cot and peered up and down the hallway, studying the heavy metal doors and staring into the security cameras. She looked at Travis's cell, hoping that he would be awake and they could talk, even if it was just about Cookie. She was surprised to find his cell empty. Maureen hoped that they sent him home. He didn't know anything at all, not even who he was.

She lay back down on her cot and put her hands behind her head and crossed her legs. She had the depressing thought that this cot in a prison cell was more comfortable than the fold-out couch she'd been sleeping on for years. For a moment Maureen wondered if she were better off in prison. They fed her actual food and she slept on a comfortable bed. The cell was even temperature controlled, unlike her cheap apartment.

She pushed those unfortunate thoughts aside and tried to piece together what happened. She was pretty sure that Herman hadn't lied about everything. Her captors were feeding her, which seemed particularly odd. But she'd been positive that she was captured by Jasper security based on the uniforms and

EMILY ECHOLS

the weapons. Was it possible Foodies were holding her? That seemed unlikely but if Jasper Industries held her why weren't they feeding her EZ Meal?

Herman was also confusing. He seemed like a bad guy who was trying to be a good guy. He'd fought Richard on returning to Harvest and then aided in her capture. Maybe he had to. Maybe if he'd returned they would have killed him if he didn't deliver her. She tried to push some of these mysteries to the back of her mind and concentrate on things that might get her out of the cell.

Maureen racked her brain trying to remember what part of the village she might be in. The Jasper Industries buildings all stood on the north side of town, near Anthony's secret collection, the opposite direction from the park and the safe house. She tried to think what building she could be in. It was a huge complex and any building could have a dungeon in a basement. It seemed plausible that *every* Jasper Industries building had a dungeon in the basement. She'd always thought they were involved in some shady dealings but now that they were kidnapping people without memories and people who knew very little, she thought that Jasper Industries was capable of anything. Maureen flipped through a mental list of people who had died or disappeared under odd circumstances. It was a very long list that included her parents.

Her parents died in a "lab accident." That was what the official report said. Maureen had asked for

144

more details. Exactly what happened? How was no one else injured? She'd thought they were chemists tweaking EZ Meal. Had there been an explosion? Had they been exposed to toxic chemicals? No one would answer her questions. The Jasper Industries officials claimed that they couldn't release all the details because her parents had been working on top-secret projects. What could be top secret about the thing that fed nearly everyone in the world?

Sam accepted their parents' deaths. Maureen never understood why. He didn't seem frustrated with the lack of details. He said that maybe they were trying to spare them the gory details. Maureen asked to see the bodies at the funeral. She simply asked for an open casket. She was told that the bodies were not in a condition to be viewed. She'd screamed and tried to pry open a coffin yelling that her parents weren't really in there. Sam had picked her up, kicking and screaming, and carried her out of the building. The funeral attendees shook their heads sadly. They chalked it up to teenage grief. Now, with what she knew, she was certain Jasper Industries had murdered them.

She wondered what her parents might have done to be murdered. Maybe they'd learned why people died so young. Maybe they'd found contaminated EZ Meal. Sam had told her they'd been involved with Foodies. Maureen could think of a million things that Jasper Industries would want to hide. She only knew the tip of the iceberg.

Sam floated in and out of her thoughts. She worried about him. She wondered if he knew she was gone, what he thought had happened to her. She wondered if she should have told him more. When she imagined him in an adjoining cell she was glad she hadn't drug him into this.

Maureen tried to think what she had done to deserve this fate. Really she'd just been talking to people and asking questions. She hadn't actually done anything, not yet anyway. She wasn't even sure what she was trying to do anymore. Things had escalated so quickly. She thought about her celebrity status. Maybe she'd done something without knowing it. Maybe Jasper Industries knew about her reputation and that was why they were interested in her. She wished she knew why everyone seemed to know who she was.

Maybe it had something to do with her parents. Maybe all these people who knew her name knew what her parents had discovered. Perhaps that's where her fame came from. Maureen's head ached with questions. She massaged her temples with the tips of her fingers. She had a hard time understanding how the sequence of events had led her here. She was positive that she was missing some key information. What was it?

Maureen stood and yelled, "What did I do? Tell me!" She stared directly at the cameras. Someone was watching. Staring directly at the camera she stood on her bed and tried to reach the vent, mostly for something to do and to get someone's attention. The ceiling was much too tall for her five-foot frame. She threw the bedclothes on the floor and tried to stand the cot up on its end. It was too unstable to climb on. She tried to pick up the bed from its end to hit the air vent. It was much too heavy for her to pick up that way.

Maureen threw the bed back down in its normal position and screamed in frustration. She heard a noise she hadn't heard before. She realized the heavy metal door was scraping against the concrete floor. It was opening. A thin dour-looking man wearing a navy and white uniform walked into the hallway. He slowly closed the door and locked it behind him. Maureen racked her brain trying to figure out what his uniform meant. Was he in the military? He walked directly to her cell. He stood in front of it and cleared his throat.

CHAPTER 16

"Master Jasper would like to invite you to supper. In an hour, Mrs. Reeves will come for you. She will take you to freshen up. Please be on your best behavior, Miss Baker," the man said in a nasal voice.

The man turned on his heels and walked away. There were a million questions going through Maureen's head but she was too stunned to speak. Which Master Jasper? James the third or the fourth? Was James Jasper Jr. still alive? Maureen doubted it. James the fourth was her age. She remembered him from school. They'd called him Jimmy. He was an entitled brat. Somehow in the age of EZ Meal he was chubby in a way that no one else was. His dirty blonde hair was always longer than regulation, hanging over his ears. Maureen shuddered at the thought of him. She'd never met James the Third. Perhaps he was more pleasant than his son.

Either way, why had one of the Jaspers taken a particular interest in her? Was that a good thing or a bad thing? Was she going to be helped or hurt by this interest? Maureen wondered what the youngest

James Jasper could possibly want with her and decided it must be his father, although she still didn't understand why he would want to see her.

Maureen didn't have much time to stew. Mrs. Reeves, a matronly woman dressed in a similar white and navy uniform showed up ahead of schedule. She actually apologized for it. "Miss Baker I apologize for arriving early. I thought you might like some extra time to freshen up after your stay here." Mrs. Reeves waved her hands around the dungeon. Two large men with bored expressions followed Mrs. Reeves. Maureen assumed they were there to keep her from trying to escape.

Mrs. Reeves unlocked her cell and actually clasped Maureen's hand in hers. Maureen was warmed by the gesture and realized it had been a while since anyone had touched her lovingly. They walked hand in hand out of the dungeon. Past the metal door was a series of dark hallways. Eventually Mrs. Reeves led her into an elevator. Maureen had heard of them but had never been in a building tall enough to use one before. All the older buildings in town had to be shorter than the old cathedral, which was no longer standing, because of some archaic rule. The Jasper Industries buildings were much newer than any other in Harvest. When the elevator doors opened Maureen gasped at the luxurious sight. Mrs. Reeves' shoes clicked on the marble tile. She led Maureen down a sumptuously decorated hallway. Marble sculptures stood on pedestals. Thick heavy tapestries hung on the walls among oil paintings of ancient ancestors. Gold molding outlined the walls. Maureen glanced up to see the painted ceiling covered in cherubs.

Mrs. Reeves led her into a room. The men followed behind. In the room stood an enormous wooden four-poster bed. Everything was velvet and gilt. The carpet felt like walking through sand it was so thick. Mrs. Reeves led her into a bathroom. The men stayed back in the bedroom. One stood watch by the door, the other by the windows.

The bathroom was larger than Maureen's entire apartment. A sunken bathtub sat in the middle of the room. Mrs. Reeves opened a cabinet, removed thick plush towels and laid them out. She went back into the bedroom, opened a heavily carved wardrobe and removed what looked like gray pajamas. "These should fit, dear. If you have a problem, tell one of these gentlemen and they'll find me." Mrs. Reeves closed the door.

Maureen started to unzip her filthy coveralls. She heard a knock on the door and Mrs. Reeves poked her head back in. "I don't mean to be crass dear but these men are going to stay out here waiting for you. I expect you to act like a lady." With that she closed the door again. Maureen heard it lock from outside. She let out a sigh. At this point a bath seemed better than freedom. She had far too many questions that needed to be answered before she could leave.

As Maureen settled into the warm, bubbly tub

she thought it felt like a scene from a fairy tale. Would Master Jasper be the beast that she had to fall in love with? She giggled to herself. At this point she thought anything was possible. Maureen frowned, worried that she was losing her grasp on reality. This wasn't a humorous situation. How long had she been gone? A few days? A week? Maureen didn't know. She had completely lost track of time.

She felt fairly certain they weren't feeding her, bathing her and dressing her in clean clothes to kill her. She couldn't figure out a motive. What was this about? The biggest question still nagged her: why her?

After her bath Maureen dressed in the new gray pajamas. They were much softer than the thick canvas of her coveralls. Maureen thought about taking her nameplate off her coveralls and affixing it to her new clothes. She felt naked without it. She dismissed the idea. She decided whatever was going to happen to her, she wouldn't need the nameplate any longer.

Newly rejuvenated she looked around the room again. There were no windows and nothing that could be used as a weapon. Maureen edited that; nothing that she knew how to use as a weapon. If she tried to pry a leg off the dressing table security would hear her before she was done. She sat at the dressing table and riffled through the single narrow drawer. Her snooping yielded a comb, a brush with a heavy metal handle and a mirror with an equally heavy handle. Maureen weighed the brush in her hand.

Was it heavy enough to use to hit someone? Then she looked at her new clothes and for the first time in her life wished she had more pockets. There was nowhere to put her potential weapons. In a moment of desperation she thrust her hand into the back of the drawer and recovered a solitary bobby pin. Maureen had read books where the heroine used one to pick a lock. She pocketed it like a magical talisman, hoping that her book knowledge might be her salvation.

Mrs. Reeves appeared at the door. She smiled when she saw Maureen with the silver brush and mirror. "Lovely, aren't they? They belonged to the Mistress." Maureen carefully returned the items to the drawer. "Please follow me." Mrs. Reeves took her by the hand again and led her out of the bathroom and the bedroom down the hall, the large men in tow. They walked through hallways that seemed miles long until the hallway opened up into a large banquet hall.

In the middle of the room was a comically long heavy wooden table. Mrs. Reeves walked Maureen past the table towards the man sitting at the head of the table. Maureen stifled a gasp. She recognized Jimmy Jasper, James Jasper the Fourth. She hadn't seen him since high school graduation. He was just as she remembered him, including his customary smirk. He was wearing the same gray pajamas that Maureen wore.

"Maureen Baker. I'm sure you remember me," Jimmy said. Maureen's manners got the best of her.

"Of course, good to see you, James."

"Please, have a seat," he motioned towards the chair beside him. Maureen sat and as she did the dour-looking man in the blue and white uniform appeared behind her and pushed in her chair.

"Oh, thank you," Maureen mumbled, not knowing the protocol.

Maureen was staring at Jimmy, trying to work out his motives. When she wasn't staring at him, her eyes darted around the room, checking on the guards and planning escape routes.

"Well, let's eat," Jimmy said. Maureen managed a slight smile. The man in the navy and white uniform appeared. He held two small silver trays, each with a crystal glass of H_2O and an EZ Meal pellet. He placed one in front of Jimmy and one in front of Maureen.

"Go on then," Jimmy Jasper encouraged. "Don't worry. We have your specs here. It's the same as the ones you take at home." Maureen wondered if this was a trick. Why feed her for days and then give her EZ Meal again? Was it poisoned? She watched as Jimmy took his pill and set the crystal glass back down on the table.

"Well? Not hungry?" he asked good-naturedly. "Maybe later then. I have something I'd like to show you or rather someone I'd like you to meet." Jimmy stood abruptly and began to walk away from the table. Maureen didn't know what was going on. She wasn't even sure if he intended for her to follow him. He walked down the long room, his slipper-like shoes shuffling on the marble floor. Maureen was confused but she stood quickly and caught up to Jimmy.

He led her down the hallway she'd walked earlier. They got back in the elevator. He pressed a button and the doors closed. Maureen wished she'd been making a better mental map of the complex. She was also surprised that no one was following them, not Mrs. Reeves, or the man in the blue uniform, or the guards. Wherever they were going she and Jimmy were going alone.

"So, Maureen. How ya been?" Jimmy asked conversationally. Does he not know I've been in a cell for the past few days? Maureen thought.

"OK," Maureen responded hesitantly. She wasn't sure how much Jimmy knew. "How have you been?"

"Me? Oh I've been grand. But there's this one problem. And my dad said your parents—I don't know, it's probably dumb but I thought maybe you could help."

"Help with what, Jimmy?" Maureen asked cautiously. The elevator stopped and the doors opened.

"We're here!" Jimmy said gleefully. Maureen followed him out of the elevator.

They appeared to be underground again. The dimly lit hallway seemed to go on forever. Large pipes crisscrossed the low ceiling. The walls were made of white-painted bricks. The floors were untreated concrete. They walked down the empty hall, Jimmy ducking under the low-hanging pipes. Finally they arrived at a metal door with no windows or markings. It appeared to be the only door on the entire floor. Jimmy pulled a large keychain out of his pocket and unlocked the door. More prisoners? Maureen wondered.

Jimmy opened the door and stepped inside.

"Gramps, I brought you a visitor," Jimmy called cheerfully. James Jasper, Jr.? Maureen thought. It couldn't be! Maureen entered the large, sterile room. It was a well-stocked lab filled with instruments Maureen couldn't identify. An elderly man in a lab coat approached them.

"Is this her?" the elderly man asked Jimmy.

"Yes, Gramps. This is Maureen Baker, the daughter of the great scientists. She's here to help you find a solution."

"Solution to what?" Maureen blurted out. "I mean, nice to meet you, sir."

"Please, call me Gramps," the old man smiled, holding out a hand for Maureen to shake. He was totally bald and his eyes seemed colorless, as though they'd lost pigmentation. He looked so fragile Maureen was afraid she'd break his hand as she took it in hers. It was freezing, like death.

"Excuse me sir. Are you James Jasper, Jr.?"

"I can't do the name justice. Please call me Gramps," he insisted. "Jimmy here says you can help me. I would love to pick your brain. What are your thoughts?"

"I'm sorry, sir, I mean Gramps but I don't think I've been fully...briefed on the situation," Maureen tried to be as polite as possible.

Gramps turned to Jimmy. "You didn't tell her?"

Jimmy shrugged. "I thought she knew."

Gramps turned back to Maureen. He put his hand on her back and guided her over to a table with a large opened book.

"You know that EZ Meal shortens our lifespan?" Maureen nodded. "I've dedicated my life to trying to learn why. I thought that maybe you — you're my last hope. I thought that because your parents were so gifted they'd told you something or you shared their gift..." His gaze left hers and settled on a large beaker on a Bunsen burner that was boiling over.

"Dang nabit! Some days I don't know why I even bother!" Gramps said walking slowly towards the beaker. Jimmy intercepted it and pulled the beaker off the heat with tongs, turned the Bunsen burner off and started to clean up the mess.

"Gramps, you know that's not true. You do it for us," Jimmy tried to assure him.

"It's a lost cause. Hopeless. It's hopeless." The old man folded his arms across his chest.

"It's not hopeless," Jimmy urged again. Gramps looked up. He unfolded his arms and turned to Maureen.

"I'm hoping that my life's work was not in vain. What can you tell me?" He looked at her with a pleading expression in his eyes. He seemed so fragile. Maureen was afraid her words might kill him.

"I'm afraid...I don't think," Maureen stumbled. "I

don't know if I can help you."

Gramps seemed distracted by something in the distance. When he turned back to Maureen his eyes were filled with confusion. "Jimmy! Who's this?" Gramps asked, shuffling away from Maureen.

"Gramps this is Maureen Baker. She's here to help. Remember?" Jimmy said gently, putting an arm around Gramps.

"I don't know her," Gramps said, the fear rising in his voice.

"She's a friend of mine," Jimmy said quietly.

A loud banging on the door startled everyone in the room. Maureen was afraid that Gramps was going to jump out of his skin.

"Open this door now!" a man's voice yelled from the other side of the door. Maureen felt certain that it was Jimmy's father, Jim Jasper, James Jasper the third.

"Shit," Jimmy said, scanning the room with a panicked expression on his face.

"What do I — what should we?" Maureen started to say. Gramps was huddled in the farthest corner of the room, his arms wrapped around himself. He appeared to be shivering. Slowly Jimmy approached the door.

"Father I," he called through the door. "It was for Gramps. I thought that maybe..."

"In ten seconds I'm having this door opened the hard way," Jim Jasper responded.

"Oh no! Don't do that. It will just upset Gramps."

Jimmy raced to the door and turned the lock, allowing his father and four security guards to enter the lab. Jim Jasper was wearing the same gray pajamas that Jimmy wore. He had Jimmy's sandy blonde hair except that he was bald on top. His face was stern, deep lines surrounded his mouth.

"Take her," Jim Jasper said almost casually, like it was an order he gave all the time. Two security guards walked swiftly over to Maureen. They deftly zip tied her hands together behind her back. Jim Jasper sighed loudly.

"Son, come," he said simply.

"But Dad, Gramps is all worked up. I should stay with him."

"Leave him. Let's go."

"We can't just leave him."

"You're lucky I'm not sending you to a cell like Miss Baker. Come."

"But Dad —" Jim Jasper made an almost imperceptible gesture and Jimmy was cut off as the other two guards took him by the arms and injected something from a hypodermic needle into his neck.

"Calm down, Son," Jim Jasper said after his son had already lost consciousness and was being carried out of the room by the two guards. Maureen wondered if this was just a normal day with the Jaspers.

"Take her back to her cell. She's not to be removed unless I come personally. I'll have to see who was in error for this incident. Perhaps Mrs. Reeves. She's always had a soft spot for that little brat."

"What's happening? Where am I?" James Jasper Jr. asked nervously. Jim Jasper ignored his father. Maureen felt the words rising up in her throat and they were out before she could stop them.

"You can't just leave him here. He needs to be cared for. There was an accident with a beaker. He could hurt himself," she said. Jim Jasper didn't look at her or acknowledge that she was speaking.

"While you're at it, gag her," he directed the guards and left the room. Maureen's taller guard locked the door behind them while the other patted his pockets, obviously searching for a gag. Jim Jasper headed to the elevators, leaving Maureen and her two guards, along with Jimmy and his two guards.

The taller guard looked at the second and said with impatience, "Are you going to do it?" The second guard said, "I don't have anything." The tall one just shrugged. All six of them squished into the elevator.

"This kid is damn heavy. Hit seven first," one of Jimmy's guards complained.

Maureen's taller guard shot him a look, telling him to be quiet. Her other guard pressed the button for the dungeon. One of Jimmy's guards readjusted Jimmy's weight and reached for the button.

"Oh come on, this kid is huge." Maureen's guard pressed another button. The taller guard shot him the same annoyed look.

The elevator doors opened while Maureen was still trying to formulate a plan. Apparently, Jimmy's guards had won the argument. The doors opened onto a hallway with marble floors. Jimmy's guards were halfway out of the elevator when the taller guard, grabbed a guard's arm and said, "Wrong floor." Jimmy's guards started to drag him back into the elevator.

Maureen heard boots on the marble. Maureen's guards let go of her arms. One peeked out of the elevator doors while the other tried to help drag Jimmy back into the elevator.

"What the hell?" one of the guards yelled.

"Press the button!" another yelled.

Maureen made her move. She threw her zip-tied hands up in the air behind her and then slammed them down on her lower back.

"Hey!" the taller guard yelled, moving towards her in the crowded elevator. Maureen threw her bound hands up again and slammed harder this time. The zip tie snapped, slicing through her wrists. She hurled herself through the elevator door, the guards grabbing at her. The door closed and the elevator left.

CHAPTER 17

Maureen found herself lying on the floor and staring face to face with Matthew Miller. He was dressed all in black, almost like the Jasper security guards. He gazed down at her with his green eyes. Time slowed. The edges of reality blurred. He took her hand and helped her to her feet. Maureen felt as though she were outside of her body, watching the action unfold. A red-haired woman jogged ahead of them and yelled, "No time for reunions! Let's go!" Time sped back up and suddenly Maureen was present again. The red-haired woman opened a door to a stairwell and the three of them ran down.

A few stories down a door opened. Two guards ran through, guns drawn. The red-haired woman punched one in the face. He fell backwards down the stairs. The first one shot his gun but the shot went wide as she kicked him in the stomach. Maureen, Matthew and the red-haired woman continued to run. A stairwell door opened and they heard shots. Richard Fischer breezed through the door with Travis in tow.

"What the hell are you waiting for?" Richard yelled, dragging Travis behind him. They ran down two more flights of stairs. Richard flung a door open and sunshine streamed into the stairwell. Maureen heard the running motor of a car. It was a large rusty van. The red-haired woman opened the back of the van and helped Richard throw Travis in the back. Maureen jumped in. Matthew and Richard jumped in behind her and started to close the doors. The red-haired woman was running around to the passenger side door when the stairwell door opened and a crowd of Jasper guards ran out. The van started to drive with the back door still open and the red-haired woman jogging beside it. The guards started shooting. The red-haired woman was shot in the shoulder.

Matthew climbed into the front seat of the van. The red-haired woman was still jogging beside them but she'd slowed down. "Pepper!" Matthew yelled to the woman, leaning out of the van and offering her his hand. Pepper sped up, running harder. The Jasper guards were running hard and close to catching up with the slow-moving van. "Pepper!" Matthew yelled again, with more emotion. She jumped a little and he grabbed her hand with one arm, pulling her closer until he could grab her by the waist and haul her inside. He slammed the passenger side door and Richard slammed the back doors closed. They heard a few more shots. Maureen expected to be followed but the guards stood and watched them drive away.

"Why are they giving up?" she asked.

"We're not worth it. They made their point," Richard replied. He put his arm around Maureen's neck and pulled her to him, kissing the top of her head. "Lamb, I'm so sorry about Herman. If I'd known — I'm glad you're safe." He smiled at her. His smile turned to a frown as he took her wrists in his hands. "What happened?"

"I broke out of zip ties."

"You know how to break out of zip ties?" Richard smiled again. "We've got a live one, folks!" he called to the others in the van. Richard moved from Maureen to Matthew and Pepper. Matthew was applying pressure to her bleeding shoulder.

"How is she?" he asked Matthew.

"She'll be fine. We'll have to dig out the bullet and she might need blood."

"I don't need blood," Pepper spat.

"If Doc says you do, you'll take it," Richard replied. "It was damn stupid of you to run to the passenger door."

Travis was huddled in a back corner of the van, mumbling to himself. Maureen approached him. "Travis? Do you know who I am?" she asked.

"No, who are you people and where are you taking me?"

Maureen glanced around the van, allowing someone with more knowledge to answer the question.

"We're your friends and we're taking you home," replied Richard. Maureen let out a breath, like she'd forgotten to breath until that moment. The world slowed back down to a normal pace. Travis seemed to relax. He sat cross-legged with his back against the van. Maureen slowly edged closer to Travis and sat beside him. She carefully reached out and patted his hand. She looked towards the front of the van and watched Matthew applying pressure to Pepper's arm. They both seemed oddly calm considering the circumstances. Maureen worried that the farm wasn't a safe place. Maybe this wasn't the first time Pepper had been shot.

She watched Matthew brush a hair off Pepper's forehead. A pang of jealously stirred in her stomach. This wasn't the reunion she'd been expecting. Richard, Pepper and Matthew conferred near the front of the van. They seemed to be having a serious conversation. Matthew glanced back at her with a concerned expression. When he realized she was looking at him, he forced a weak smile.

Maureen tried to look away. She tried to look out the windows, watching the route the van took them but she just couldn't. She studied Matthew. He looked much older than she remembered. It had only been two years since she'd last seen him. Maybe it was because he was more muscular and he needed a shave. He looked commanding and capable. Maureen felt small and bumbling in comparison. She tried to imagine what would have happened to her if Pepper and Matthew hadn't showed up.

She looked down at her wrists. She was surprised

that they still didn't hurt. She knew it was adrenalin and that eventually she would feel pain. Riding in the van with Travis, Matthew and Richard felt surreal. They had been characters in a story that she concocted in her head. It was difficult for her to comprehend that this was really happening.

The van stopped. It didn't seem that they were far enough away from the village to be at the farm. Maureen chalked it up to not being familiar with estimating driving distances. Surely they were farther from Harvest than they seemed. Richard opened the side door. Matthew tried to help Pepper out of the van. "I got it, Matt!" she snapped. Richard gave Matthew an subtle command with his eyes and he followed her out of the van. Richard looked back at Maureen and Travis.

"This is your stop, too. Health lodge," Richard said. Maureen nudged Travis and they both climbed out of the van. "Davy, I'll take the vehicle. Show Maureen and Travis where to go."

"But Matt," the driver protested.

"Is busy with Pepper. Thanks. Good work."

Davy got out of the van and Maureen noticed him for the first time. He was a dark, barrel-chested bearded man. He thrust out his hand, "Davy Cook."

Maureen shook it. "Maureen Baker. Good to meet you. Thank you."

Davy smiled. "We all know who you are." Davy led the way to the health lodge.

CHAPTER 18

The health lodge was a log cabin. It had two separate sections, each divided into two rooms with a breezeway between the sections. Rocking chairs and a wooden table sat in the breezeway. Maureen thought it looked like paradise. Before they walked inside they heard a woman cursing loudly. Travis cowered behind Maureen. "Don't be afraid. It's just Pepper," Davy said. He leaned in conspiratorially. "She's not much different when she hasn't been shot."

Davy led them inside. There was a row of four wooden beds with bright white sheets on them. "Have a seat. Rosemary will be here soon." Maureen sat down on a bed. Travis sat next to her.

"Davy?" Travis's voice surprised them both. "Are we safe here?" Travis asked. Davy paused for what felt like too long to Maureen.

"Yes, you're safe here." Davy closed the door and left them. As soon as the door closed Maureen let out a gasping sob that shook her entire body. Travis put his arm around her and pulled her into a hug. Maureen shook and Travis held her. After a moment Maureen realized he was crying too. She wrapped her arms around him and they held each other and cried.

The door squeaked open, startling them. "Oh my sweet dears! I didn't think you were seriously injured. I'm so sorry." A woman rushed towards them. She had a long brown braid that hung down her back, a sharp little nose and a large scar down the side of her right cheek. She was wearing a modest robin's egg blue cotton dress. "I'm Rosemary. Tell me where it hurts."

"Everywhere," Maureen answered breathlessly.

"Everywhere? I thought it was just your wrists. What happened?" Rosemary looked Maureen over with concern, looking for injuries, finally realizing that Maureen was reacting to the stress of her escape. Rosemary pulled them both into a motherly hug. "You're safe now. You're home. I know it's frightening. I went through something similar." She squeezed tighter right before she released them both. "Would you like a drink of water?" Maureen and Travis both nodded. Rosemary poured them water from a pitcher and handed them each a glass. "Now let's have a look at those wrists."

Rosemary had Maureen's wrists cleaned and bandaged in no time. She explained to Maureen and Travis what was going to happen to him. There were some drugs they were going to give him that would help him recover his memories. He would also play games and talk with Rosemary. Because they wouldn't know day to day how much he would remember he was going to stay at the health lodge, partly for his own safety. Travis seemed to accept and understand all of this.

Rosemary explained that she needed to do some preliminary tests with Travis to set a baseline for what he remembered. She also needed to give him the first dose of the medicine. She sent Maureen across the way to another cabin to get something to eat. She promised that Travis would follow her shortly. As Maureen stepped out of the cabin she saw Pepper coming out of the cabin, across the breeze-way, with Matthew following close behind.

"Pepper, get back here," Matthew called.

"No. I'm fine." Pepper marched off.

"Matthew!" Maureen called to him.

He glanced at Maureen without smiling. "Not now. Pepper is refusing pain medication and she's going to regret it later." Matthew jogged after Pepper.

Maureen took her eyes off them and walked to the cabin that Rosemary had directed her. It was very warm in the cabin. Maureen realized it was because of a large metal wood-burning stove on one wall. At this time of year it was nearly stifling. Davy was standing at the stove stirring something in a large pot. It smelled heavenly, although Maureen didn't have words to describe the cooking food. She realized that her food notes were not helpful when it came to smells and tastes.

"Come in. Come in." Davy motioned towards a long rectangular table with benches. Maureen sat. Although Maureen had just come from James Jasper's banquet table this was the loveliest table she'd ever seen. The top of the large wooden table was covered in knots. Dents and grooves covered its surface. Looking at the table, Maureen tried to imagine the history it contained, the number of meals shared across it. Davy spooned food from a pot on the stove into a bowl and set it before Maureen. He sat down next to Maureen.

"Hungry?" he asked affably.

"Despite everything, yes. I barely ate anything at...the house," Maureen wasn't sure what to call the Jasper compound.

Maureen greedily shoveled spoonful after spoonful of stew into her mouth, burning her tongue. It was filled with small pieces of meat and brightly colored vegetables. Maureen tried to identify the vegetables. It was harder when they were cut into small pieces. Carrots and potatoes were the only ones she was confident of.

"Forgot the bread!" Davy said. He stood and ripped a large hunk of bread off a loaf that was wrapped in a dishtowel on the table beside the stove. He handed it to Maureen. It looked exactly like the bread Herman had given her. She wanted to ask about Herman but decided this wasn't the time. As she ate, she gazed around the house. One wall was lined with large metal bins and shelves filled with glass and clay containers. Davy handed her a glass of water.

"Well, stay put for a bit. Finish eating. Richard will be here soon."

"You're going?" Maureen asked, suddenly feeling a

little lost.

"Yeah, I got things to do. Sorry to leave you to eat alone. You'll see it's not our way. Probably the only time it'll ever happen. Richard'll be here soon." Davy left.

Maureen took a few more large bites of stew and ripped off a large hunk of bread. She stood, deciding that she was going exploring. She walked to the door and started to push it out and realized that someone was pulling out from the outside. She let go and the door opened. Richard Fischer stepped inside. Maureen returned to the table and sat at her unfinished bowl of stew. Richard joined her at the table.

"Glad to see you're enjoying the stew. That Mary's a fine cook, isn't she?" Maureen didn't know who Mary was. She nodded politely.

"Well, Lamb, welcome home!" A wide grin spread across Richard's face. He walked over to Maureen and stood next to her, waiting for her to stand so he could hug her. Even though she was uncomfortable, Maureen obliged. Maureen was waiting for an explanation that was very long in coming. Richard released her and sat back down.

"Is it just like you remember it? OK, well maybe not just like. We've made some great improvements."

"I don't know what you're talking about," Maureen interrupted. Richard's face fell.

"Oh, you really don't? I thought that was all...Oh. Well. Then I think I have some apologies to make and some explanations to give. I'm very sorry. I didn't know."

Richard seemed to be thinking about how to proceed.

"Give me a moment," he excused himself. Maureen could hear him speaking to someone right outside of the cabin. Maybe her ignorance had changed plans. He returned to the table. "Maureen, I knew you as a little girl. In fact, you were born here."

Maureen's jaw dropped. "No, no. I was born in the village. I've always lived in the village. I would remember..." Maureen felt panic rising in her throat like a scream.

"You were very young when your parents took you to the village. They didn't want to force this lifestyle on you. We had a few hard winters that led to some food shortages. Many people left during those years. Your parents never gave up on the dream of food self-sufficiency but they wanted you and your brother to have enough. However, as chemists at Jasper Industries they learned some terrible things. They wanted to take you away but—but they were not able to."

Maureen noticed he didn't say that they died. A lot of people used euphemisms for death. That wasn't unusual but Richard didn't even do that. Maureen tried not to read too much into that statement.

"What kind of terrible things?" Maureen asked. Once she said it, she wondered why she'd formulated that particular question into words while a hundred others swirled around in her head.

"We don't need to get into all that now," Richard started.

"Please tell me."

"Your parents were working with James Jasper Jr. trying to figure out why EZ Meal shortened lives. He wanted to fix it but his son told him it was a pipe dream. He said it didn't matter and refused to let your parents work on the solution. But they did anyway. Your parents figured out what was wrong with EZ Meal and told him they'd discovered the fix."

"They figured it out?! We have to tell James Jasper Jr.! He needs to know. What happened to their research?"

"Gone. It was destroyed. But we still have their personal notes."

"What are you waiting for? Go tell Jasper Industries how to fix it!" Maureen said angrily.

"Jim Jasper won't listen. The time isn't right."

"The time isn't right? What does that mean?"

"Maureen, we actually think the answer is not to fix EZ Meal. We think the answer lies in food."

"You're bringing food back to everyone?"

"Well, there are a lot of difficulties in that scenario..."

"You know how to fix EZ Meal but you're not going to? You think food is the answer but you're not going to share it with everyone?" Maureen was aghast.

"We don't have the capabilities...we can barely sustain ourselves. We're working on a permanent solution but for now..."

"For now you're just letting people die of old age at sixty?"

"It's complicated. We can talk more about it later." Richard paused, letting the conversation die. "We are thrilled beyond belief to have you back, Lamb. Welcome home."

"This isn't my home. I have a lot of questions that need answers," Maureen said a little angrily. She hadn't forgotten what Richard had just said.

"It used to be. It can be again. We'll tell you everything in time. I have a special surprise for you. Come with me."

CHAPTER 19

Richard led Maureen to another cabin. This one was much larger than the first. A crowd was assembled in the cabin. Maureen scanned the crowd for the Foodies she knew. There was no sign of Matthew, Pepper or Davy.

A heavily pregnant woman came forward out of the crowd. She could have been Maureen's aunt. They had the same thick, curly dark brown hair. She clasped Maureen's hand between hers. "Maureen Baker!" The woman smiled at her as though studying her. "Welcome. I'm Ginger. There is something we do for most new recruits. Well, I guess this is more of a homecoming, isn't it?" as she said that Ginger pulled Maureen into a warm hug that was made awkward by Ginger's large belly. When she pulled away Maureen thought Ginger was crying. "We'd like to show you something." Ginger placed a small card in Maureen's hand. Maureen held the small browned card in her hand carefully. She peered at the words, trying to make out the cramped script.

Grandma Dottie's Molasses Cookies

¾ c melted oleo
¼ c molasses
1 egg
1 c sugar
2 t baking soda
2 c flour
½ t cloves
½ t ginger
1 t cinnamon
½ t salt

Beat butter, molasses, egg and sugar. Sift dry ingredients. Add to first mixture and beat well. Chill three hours or more. Roll into balls, dip in sugar. Place on greased cookies sheet, flatten with a fork. Bake at 375 degrees 8-10 min.

"What does oleo mean?" Maureen asked.

"It's another word for butter," Ginger said.

"What about the ts and cs? What do those mean?"

"They're standard measurements. It tells you how much to use. The c is for cup and the small t is a teaspoon. A big T is a tablespoon, a larger measurement," Ginger told her gently.

"It's like a lost language," Maureen breathed.

"It is," Ginger agreed.

Maureen noticed the title at the top. "Who was Grandma Dottie?"

"We don't know," an older woman said. "We think she was very influential. We have many of her recipes."

"She was a great cook," another man said, with reverence.

"Have you made these? What are they like?" Maureen asked. Laughter erupted around the room.

"Of course we've made them!" the older woman exclaimed.

"It took us a long time to identify and find all the spices. They taste like heaven." Ginger handed Maureen a golden brown disk about two inches in diameter. It seemed to sparkle like a jewel in the light. "Go on, try it," Ginger urged gently.

Maureen sniffed. "It smells like Christmas!" she exclaimed. "Wait, why did I say that?" Maureen surprised herself by using the archaic word. She had an idea of what Christmas used to be from reading books but had never celebrated it.

"Because something in you knows. Something in your remembers," Ginger urged. "Go on."

Maureen took a bite. It not only smelled like Christmas, it tasted like Christmas too. It was sweet and spicy, crunchy on the outside but chewy on the inside. It broke off easily in her mouth. She chewed slowly.

"These are...oh my gosh...this is...life-changing!" Maureen exclaimed.

"I know they are," Ginger said. "Now you understand why we're here."

"And that's just one cookie. Imagine what other foods taste like. Grandma Dottie left a whole treasure trove of recipes behind," a man added.

Maureen looked up at Ginger. "Go on. Eat the rest. We can make more," Ginger said. It was permission to eat the rest of the cookie. Maureen hadn't been exaggerating when she said it was life-changing. That first crumb of bread had been enough to convince her that there was no way she could go back. But this cookie, this cookie was a call to arms. This cookie was the first shot in the battle that Maureen was going to fight for food.

Maureen didn't know what to do with her new realization. Ginger sensed that Maureen couldn't speak and handed her another cookie. She ate it gladly. Ginger almost whispered in Maureen's ear, "Have they told you the news?"

"That I was born here?"

Ginger looked around the room, trying to make eye contact with someone besides Maureen.

"Then no?" Ginger finally managed.

Maureen thought that coming to the farm would be the end of secrets. What were they still keeping from her? Ginger smiled at Maureen and handed her another cookie. "I'll be right back," she said as she stormed out of the cabin.

"Do you have more recipes I could look at? I have some too..." Maureen pulled the small recipe book out from under her shirt. She was thankful that it had survived her escape, carefully lodged in her ample cleavage. The older woman came forward to see it. Her eyes lit up and she smiled wide.

"Oh, this is a wonderful find! We'll have to try these. Is this a family book?"

"It was my great-grandmother's. It was written right before The Collapse."

"This is good news." The woman continued to turn pages and smile.

A loud ruckus started outside the cabin. Maureen recognized Ginger's sweet voice yelling at the top of her lungs.

"How could you do this to her? She doesn't know! How do you think she's going to react when we tell her? You have to tell her!"

A rumble of conversation erupted in the cabin. Maureen imagined she was arguing with Richard. She hated people talking about her like she was an idiot or a child. She knew they were still keeping things from her but what could it be? The door opened and Richard appeared. The cabin fell silent. He said, "Maureen come with me," as though she was being called to the principal's office. Maureen searched Ginger's face. She wiped her angry tears away and tried to smile. Maureen was worried that she was going to be told bad news. This whole time she thought there was more to the story but she never imagined it was bad.

Richard started walking away from Ginger and the cabin. Maureen followed. He was walking quickly and she felt herself almost jogging to keep up. When Maureen caught up to him she realized he'd been talking, thinking she was right behind him. "Naturally we knew we should tell you but we wanted the timing to be right. I knew it would be quite a shock and I just didn't want to rush into things. But no, I think that Ginger is right. We need to tell you. Many of us thought you would find out for yourself. You're a resourceful young woman. You found us, didn't you?"

Maureen thought of mentioning the fact that she didn't find them, she was rescued but decided against it. Maureen slowed a bit climbing up a large grassy hill. Richard didn't miss a beat so she fell behind again. She thought they must have walked clear across sector eight and she was right. They were in sector nine, which she discovered as she caught back up to Richard saying, "Sector nine, as you can see is very similar to sector eight. In fact, all the sectors in my care are quite alike." It was like he was giving the guided tour. Maureen wondered if he continued to talk because he was nervous.

Finally Richard stood still beside a cabin. "I'll return," he said simply and slipped inside. Maureen felt that a lot of things seemed to happen behind her back. She heard a gasp from inside the cabin. A woman and a man came running out with Richard trailing them. Maureen recognized the man and woman but it was impossible. She stared. Maureen couldn't be sure who they were until the woman came running up to her and hugged her. It was her mother's hug. It was her mother's scent. It was her mother's curly dark hair against her face. It was her mother. Her father was close behind. He hugged them both. All three of them stood in a huddle, weeping for an eternity.

Maureen's head swam. Her parents were alive! The last four years were full of lies but whose lies? Jasper Industries? Her own parents? Why would they leave her? Why would they keep it a secret?

"But how?" Maureen was finally able to choke out. "Does Sam know?"

"Come inside and we'll talk," her mother said as she put her arm around Maureen and led her inside the cabin. They sat at the table. "I just made some tea, would you like some?" her mother asked and then started to cry again. She collapsed onto the dirt floor. "I can't believe you're really here," she said. Maureen went to her mother and sat on the floor.

"I can't believe *you're* really here," Maureen responded, hugging her mother tightly. She put her nose to her mother's head and sniffed. It smelled like her childhood, like every happy memory she possessed. Her father came over to the weeping women on the floor.

"Come, let's sit," he gently suggested. Maureen and her mother sat at the table while Bill Baker poured three cups of tea. Maureen dragged her thumb across the brown glaze on the mug, not knowing what to say. Her father spoke first.

"Darling, we didn't know what else to do. If we hadn't left when we did, we'd be..."

"We'd be dead," her mother interrupted. "They

were going to kill us. It was the only way."

"We couldn't take you with us. It was too big of a risk."

"Yes and it wasn't time."

"We knew you would come." Her father smiled proudly.

Maureen still felt that they were leaving too much out. "But how? What, what happened? What did you do? Why were they going to kill you? And I was born here? What happened? Please tell me everything." Nicole Baker smiled. She put her hand on Maureen's.

"It is wonderful to see you. I missed you so, so much. This may be too much for one day. Are you tired?"

"Mom, please tell me. Tell me something."

"You were born here. So was Sam," Bill began. "We defected shortly after we got married. This is the life we wanted for you. But things got bad in Harvest. We started to hear things. We were worried and we thought maybe we could help."

"News from Harvest and a few bad winters here when you were young brought us back to the village."

"We started working for Jasper Industries because we thought we could make it better but what we found out..."

"It was just too much. We were going to go public with what we learned."

"That EZ Meal kills people," Maureen interrupted. Nicole smiled, obviously proud of her daughter.

"I'm glad you know. Yes, but word got out and our only option was to escape. We've been doing what we can from here ever since," Nicole said.

"And Sam? Why doesn't he remember this place?" Maureen asked. Her parents exchanged a glance.

"You know, I think he does but maybe he's not ready or he's afraid," her mother replied carefully.

"Mom, how can you leave him there? He's your son! How could you leave either of us there?"

"Maureen, it's not that simple," Bill said. "I know it hurts to say but this is bigger than any of us. We're no use dead. Sam is safe for now."

"But you're his parents!"

"Sweetheart, we know and that's why we're letting him decide."

"You never contacted us..." Maureen started to cry. Her mother put her arm around her.

"We couldn't. It was too dangerous. Don't be sad about the past. Be happy that you're with us now."

Maureen finally lifted the mug to her lips and took a sip of the lukewarm mint tea. The tea was comforting in a way Maureen couldn't explain. It was as though tea always comforted her. It felt so reassuring. And yet she'd only had tea a handful of times. She felt like she was recovering memories of things she'd never done and people she'd never met. She was re-learning her life. She was Maureen Baker, she was a Foodie and her parents were alive. The happiness and surprise pushed the anger into a small corner of her mind. Her parents were right, this was bigger than them and she was ready to help. She took another sip of tea and set the mug down on the table. "Tell me what we're doing to change the world."

CHAPTER 20

Maureen awoke the next morning in the loft of her parents' cabin. She kicked off a red and white quilt. It was getting warm. The night before, her mother had laid out some more suitable clothes for her. Maureen quietly dressed in a simple cotton calico dress. She slipped on the soft, leather shoes. She contentedly wiggled her toes inside of her shoes. She pulled her hair back into a ponytail and climbed down the ladder.

Her parents were already at the table enjoying breakfast. Her mother poured her some tea and filled her bowl with oatmeal. Maureen didn't have words for the joy she felt in sharing a meal with her parents. It was the first meal she could remember eating with them. A warm feeling rose up from her belly and settled in her chest. It was a feeling Maureen hoped she wouldn't lose.

Maureen was surprised how quickly she settled back into life with her parents. After the initial shock of seeing them still alive she felt like no time had passed. The night before they'd told her that they had duties they needed to attend to and Maureen didn't think about protesting. She wanted to talk to Matthew, anyway.

After breakfast she started the trek to sector eight in search of Matthew Miller. As she walked by people stopped and stared. Some pointed. She heard people murmuring "Maureen Baker." She tried to think of herself as a celebrity but really it just made her nervous. She knew the basics but was convinced that she was still missing some big pieces of the puzzle. She tried to push the voices out of her head and simply enjoy the warm sun on her face as she walked across the fields. She found Matthew talking to Richard in front of the large cabin she'd eaten molasses cookies in the night before. The men grew silent as she approached.

"Maureen, good morning," Richard greeted her.

"Good morning. May I speak to Matthew or are you in the middle of something?"

"He's all yours," Richard responded. After the exchange Maureen wondered why she hadn't asked Matthew but it seemed the appropriate thing to do.

Richard walked away from the pair. Maureen gazed up at Matthew. He was strangely intimidating in his plaid shirt and brown work pants. He still hadn't shaved. Maureen wondered if he was growing a beard like so many of the men she'd seen on the farm. He didn't seem pleased to see her. His eyes darted around, as though searching for an escape route.

"Matthew, I—" Maureen began. Matthew pulled

her into an intense hug, his large body enfolding hers.

"Maureen," he whispered into the top of her head. He clung to her like a frightened child. Maureen wasn't sure how to react but was surprised when tears sprung to her eyes. Matthew released her and brushed his eyes with the back of his hand and sniffled loudly. Maureen wiped her face with both hands. Something like embarrassment crossed Matthew's face and then it grew stoic again.

"It's good to see you, old friend. I'm glad that you're here," he said rather formally.

"Matthew, I just think," Maureen tried again.

"I'll see you at the meeting tonight," he said simply and walked away. What meeting? Maureen thought. There was still so much she didn't know. Matthew seemed so changed. He knew how to deal with gunshot wounds and chased after women trying to administer pain medication. He was part of a rescue mission. She worried that they wouldn't even be friends anymore but then she thought about her own transformation. Maybe they just needed a little time.

She gazed out at the fields. She saw people with baskets on their shoulders carrying things into cabins. She could see row after row of people harvesting late summer vegetables. She was fascinated by the sight of the people in the fields and desired to join them. If her parents had never moved them to Harvest she would be one of the people out in the fields, harvesting right now, or at least that was what she imagined. Maureen realized she'd been staring for a long time. She grew embarrassed and felt lazy for not doing anything while everyone else worked. She remembered that her mother was canning with a large group of women that day while her father harvested okra. She thought about walking back to their cabin and then realized that they wouldn't be in the cabin and she didn't know how to find them.

Not knowing what else to do, Maureen opened the door and walked into the large cabin. She was relieved to see Ginger at the table. Ginger's face lit up when she saw her. "Maureen! Come join us! We're baking bread. You can help."

"I don't know anything about bread, I mean anything at all..." Maureen stammered, afraid of being in the way.

"We'll teach you. You'll need to learn anyway," Ginger said. "Maureen, this is my sister, Holly and this is my sister-in-law, Summer." Maureen turned to the women. Holly looked very much like Ginger. She had the same tightly curled dark hair. Summer looked just the way Maureen imagined someone named Summer ought to. She was tall and lithe with long, straight blonde hair. "This is Maureen Baker," Ginger said to the other women. Maureen saw recognition in the women's faces. Holly hugged her tightly.

"Maureen, it is so good to meet you," Holly said. Summer smiled shyly.

"It's so good to have you," Summer said in a little sing-song voice.

"Back to work!" Ginger said. Holly and Summer returned to their floured boards. They were each kneading a loaf of bread. Loaves of bread were strewn around the kitchen in varying stages of doneness. Some were right out of the oven, filling the air with a pleasant, sweet smell. Others were rising under dishtowels in bowls. Others still sat on the table. Some of the loaves were smooth and white while others were shades of brown, some were even black. The darker loaves looked coarser, some had what appeared to be seeds dotting them. Even their shapes varied. Most were round or rectangular. Some were long and thin, like snakes, Maureen thought. One loaf Summer was braiding intricately.

"What shall I do?" Maureen asked.

"Knead this one for me, while I check the ones in the oven," Ginger said.

"What does that mean?" Maureen asked.

"I'm sorry. I forgot. We learn this at a young age. It's easier if I demonstrate."

Ginger lifted the lump of dough with one hand and took a handful of a brown powder with the other and spread it on the table. She put the dough down and folded it in half. Then she turned it and folded it in half again. She pressed down on it with the heel of her hand.

"Like that," she said. "The flour prevents it from sticking to the table. Holly will keep an eye on you and tell you when it's done."

"OK," Maureen said, hesitantly.

"You can't mess it up," Holly said. "The only thing you could do wrong would be to knead it for too long but I'll watch you."

Maureen held the brown lump of dough in her hands. It was heavier than she'd imagined it would be. She put it on the table and folded it in half and pushed it down with the heel of her hand, just as Ginger had.

"Good, just like that," Holly encouraged.

Maureen was surprised that she liked the feel of the dough in her hands. She enjoyed the smooth texture and the slight stickiness. She was also surprised that it was warm. She turned it and folded it in half again, pushing it down with her hand. Minutes ticked by as Maureen turned, folded and pushed down, turned, folded and pushed down. Her arms started to tire. It became harder and harder to push it down as the structure of the dough changed.

"That's good," Holly said finally, poking her finger into the dough. Maureen saw the dent bounce back almost instantly. Holly put the dough into a pan and covered it with a clean dishtowel. "Here's another," she passed Maureen another lump of dough.

"Do you do this all day?" Maureen asked.

"Just about," Summer said. "We eat a lot of bread."

Maureen watched as Ginger pulled loaves of bread from the oven and put new ones in. Holly lifted a dishcloth and poked at a round, white orb of dough. Holly punched it back down and re-covered it. After hours of kneading Holly showed Maureen how her loaves had risen. Maureen was entranced and asked what made it rise like magic. She spent the rest of the afternoon learning all there was to know about bread.

They worked until the light faded in the cabin and Holly lit a lamp. Ginger encouraged Maureen to go eat dinner with her parents, adding that they would see her that evening at the meeting. Maureen was too hungry to ask about the meeting. She walked out of the baking cabin and towards the edge of sector nine to her parents' cabin.

Her mother had cooked a vegetable hash that Maureen could smell from outside the cabin. She sat at the table and had a pleasant meal with her parents, telling them about her adventures with bread and hearing about canning and harvesting. Her mother said she'd have to can with them the next day to learn all about it. When they were nearly done eating Maureen remembered she'd meant to ask them about the meeting.

"People keep talking about a meeting tonight. What is it?" she asked.

"Oh, it's just the monthly Council Meeting," Bill said.

"You really need to remember that I have no idea what that means," Maureen said.

"Oh honey, you're right. We keep forgetting. I still can't believe we abandoned you this morning. We'll work on it," Nicole promised. "Once a month we all meet together to make decisions for the farm. Everyone attends and every person over thirteen gets a vote. Tonight is going to be special because they're going to introduce you." Maureen blushed, uncomfortable.

"Who's in charge?" Maureen asked.

"Richard Fischer, for now," Bill said.

"What do you mean, 'for now'?"

"We're having elections soon and he's at his term limit. Someone else will be Steward soon."

"Is the Steward always a man?"

"Not always but usually," Bill said.

"We're still fighting patriarchy like everyone else," Nicole added with a grin.

"What are the Steward's duties?"

"We can explain all the specifics later. We should be leaving soon if we're going to make it to the meeting on time," Bill said. He rose, picking up Nicole and Maureen's plates. He carried them to the sink. He pumped water into the sink and washed the dishes, placing them on a drying rack on the counter. Maureen found herself staring again. Everything surrounding food preparation was hypnotizing even dish washing. Today she had learned that people on the farm spent most of their time in food production. It seemed like a full-time job. Maureen wondered when they had time for other things.

CHAPTER 21

By the time Maureen and her parents set out for the Council Meeting it was nearly dark. Nicole carried a kerosene lantern. They walked back to sector eight. Maureen thought that all the action seemed to happen in sector eight and couldn't understand why someone would choose to live anywhere else. She had no idea how house placement was chosen or if it was a personal choice. She added that to her mental list of questions to ask later. Maureen wondered where the meeting would be. She hadn't see a building large enough to house all the people she imagined lived on the farm.

They walked farther into sector eight than she'd been before. They arrived at a large wooden structure with a metal roof and open sides. It was filled with wooden benches. Other families had already assembled and were seated on the benches. Maureen thought that by the size of the building there were probably fewer families than she had imagined. There were only about fifty families, a few hundred people in all. There also weren't nearly as many children as Maureen had imagined. Maybe many of the younger families had made the same decision her parents had.

She saw a few benches lining the front edge of the pavilion. Richard sat on the middle bench. Matthew and Pepper flanked him with Davy beside Pepper. Maureen couldn't decide if that meant they were also ranking individuals or if they were there to report about their mission. She sat with her parents in the first row that had been reserved for them. As darkness settled on them, one by one, little kerosene lanterns were lit and hung by the rafters.

Maureen was anxious but she couldn't decide why. Richard banged a gavel on a wooden podium. The chattering voices stopped mid-sentence.

"Peace be with you," Richard said.

"And also with you," the crowd responded. The sound of everyone speaking in unison like that gave Maureen goose bumps.

"I call this meeting of sectors eight through twelve to order," Richard said. "Our rescue mission was successful. We now have Maureen Baker and Travis Carpenter safely among us. Travis's memory retrieval treatments are going well, although it will be weeks until he remembers anything from before. Maureen is here with her parents." Richard motioned for her to stand. Maureen stood slowly and turned to face the crowd. Applause erupted from the center of the crowd. Maureen couldn't understand it. Were they cheering for the successful mission? Were they cheering for her in some way? She sat quickly, embarrassed.

"Elections are upon us. Tonight we need to finalize our candidates. I have nominated Matthew Miller as a suitable Steward. Are there any other nominations?" Richard continued.

Maureen's jaw dropped. Maybe that was why Matthew acted so strange; he was training to be Richard Fischer. Goose bumps covered Maureen's arms anew. She felt a trickle of cold sweat dripping down the center of her back. She grew agitated. Her knee started bouncing without her consent. She heard a noise that sounded like metal cogs slamming against each other. She swiveled her head, waiting for others to react to the noise. She realized it was the sound of her own heart thwacking in her chest. Something felt wrong but she couldn't put it into words. She felt something like a hand at her back and before she knew what she was doing Maureen stood.

"I nominate myself," Maureen said loudly and clearly though her knees were knocking.

"Maureen? Did you say you want to nominate yourself for Steward?" Richard asked.

"Yes."

"I think that's a wonderful ambition but I'm afraid only citizens can run for Steward and I don't think you know enough about the farm to be in charge of it at this point..."

"She's a citizen," Ginger said loudly, standing on the outer edge of the pavilion. "She was born here. She's more of a citizen than Matthew Miller, forgive me."

"Now Ginger, you know that Matthew has gone through intensive training. We all agreed he could run as a citizen..."

"Did we vote on that?" Ginger asked.

"I don't think we did," a short, balding man said, standing.

"Clearly, I wouldn't be nominating him if we hadn't voted on it..." Richard stammered.

"I say let her run!" shouted the short man. A crowd of people around him cheered. Maureen had never seen him before and wondered why he was taking her side. She also didn't know why she'd stood up in the first place. And why would she run against Matthew? Matthew was wonderful, or Matthew had been wonderful. Maureen didn't know anything about him anymore. Something had compelled her to stand and now that people were supporting her candidacy she felt her confidence grow.

"Now, now. Let's all calm down," Richard urged as the cheering crowd continued to expand. It took Maureen a moment to hear what they were chanting: Baker. Maureen's heart swelled.

"Just let her run! What could it hurt?" Maureen turned to see an elderly man standing. The sight of him standing silenced the chants. His thin hair was snow white and he had deep lines across his brown face. He seemed to be missing several important teeth.

"Bird, we can't just change the rules because Maureen is— a beloved member of our community."

"We ain't changin' any rules. She's a citizen. She can run. You're the one changin' rules," Bird replied. He whistled through his missing front teeth when he talked.

Richard threw up his hands. "OK, fine. Why not?" He turned back to Maureen. "Do you officially announce your candidacy for Steward of sectors eight through twelve?"

"I do," Maureen said with more confidence than she felt.

"All right then," Richard said, trying to sound neutral but clearly unhappy with the course of events. "Are there any other nominations? Does anyone want to nominate Dilly Mason?"

Maureen knew from her conversations with Holly, Ginger and Summer that Dilly Mason was a four-year-old little girl. Snickers arose from the crowd. Some people tried to laugh politely at the inappropriate joke. Maureen couldn't decide why Richard felt so threatened by her.

"Wilford Brewer, weren't you thinking about running?" Richard asked, addressing a man in the crowd.

A man in a bowler hat stood. "I was a thinkin' about it but now that Maureen has announced her candidacy I don't reckon I'll run," he said smiling. Richard visibly tried to compose himself.

"We need to talk about the corn harvest," Richard began. The rest of the meeting was a blur of food talk that Maureen couldn't follow. People stood to give harvest reports. Ginger stood and spoke of bread with names that were still a tangled web in Maureen's head. They voted on what to plant more of next year, what to plant less of, what to try for the first time. They voted on how many goats to slaughter. Nearly every detail of their communal life was decided together, under this metal roof. Maureen was impressed that they shared so much responsibility.

"If there is no other business," Richard began.

The old toothless man stood. "Don't you think we oughter talk about The Decision again?" Bird asked.

"No, I think that is something that we're not prepared to approach at this time. We'll..."

"It's been six months. We said in six months time..." As Bird interrupted Richard a gasp blew through the crowd. It was clearly a breach in etiquette.

"Bird, you are out of order. We will discuss it at a later date," Richard said, cutting him off.

Wilford Brewer stood. "I believe that Bird is right. We said six months and that were in March. It's time we talked again."

"Next meeting," Richard assured them. "It's getting late. We've already gone longer than usual."

"I reckon we oughter talk about it now," Bird insisted.

"Another day!" Richard said, very close to a yell. "Let us close the meeting with our traditional song." He said it quickly, to keep anyone from interrupting him. Maureen was surprised that once Richard said that no one else argued. The crowd stood and every-one held hands and they sang:

All creatures of our God and King
Lift up your voice and with us sing,
Alleluia! Alleluia!
Thou burning sun with golden beam,
Thou silver moon with softer gleam!

O praise Him! O praise Him!
Alleluia! Alleluia! Alleluia!

Thou rushing wind that art so strong
Ye clouds that sail in Heaven along,
O praise Him! Alleluia!
Thou rising moon, in praise rejoice,
Ye lights of evening, find a voice!

O praise Him! O praise Him!
Alleluia! Alleluia! Alleluia!

Thou flowing water, pure and clear,
Make music for thy Lord to hear,
O praise Him! Alleluia!
Thou fire so masterful and bright,
That givest man both warmth and light.

O praise Him! O praise Him!
Alleluia! Alleluia! Alleluia!

Dear mother earth, who day by day

Unfoldest blessings on our way,
O praise Him! Alleluia!
The flowers and fruits that in thee grow,
Let them His glory also show.

O praise Him! O praise Him!
Alleluia! Alleluia! Alleluia!

Maureen didn't understand all the words but something deep inside of her seemed to. She felt warmed by the words. Later on their walk home she tried to ask her mother about the song. She just said it was a long tradition to end the meetings with that song. The conversation ended there because her father was much too upset with her to let her chat about whatever she chose.

"I can't believe you did that. What were you thinking? And to run against Matthew, your friend? Why would you do that?" Bill was talking much too quickly for her to respond. "Why? Why would you talk to Richard that way? Are you ungrateful for all that he has done for you? You've changed a lot in the last few years. My daughter would never do something like that."

Maureen listened, disinterested. She knew her father didn't expect her to answer. She still didn't know what had led her to stand and nominate herself to be the leader of a place she was only just beginning to learn about but she knew by everyone's reaction that it had been the right thing to do. She knew it the same way that although she'd never kneaded bread before her hands seemed to remember how, the way that she knew the molasses cookies tasted like Christmas and the way she knew that was an important song.

CHAPTER 22

Early the next morning there was a soft knock on the cabin door. It wasn't yet dawn and Maureen's parents were not awake. Maureen had slept fitfully. She'd been running through the events of the meeting over and over. She tried to remember every word said, trying to piece together what she knew. She was laying awake when she heard the knock. She quickly and carefully made her way down the ladder from the loft. She opened the door. It was Bird, the old toothless man.

"I reckon we oughter talk," he said. Maureen could hear her parents starting to stir in the other room. She wrapped her father's canvas jacket around her shoulders and followed Bird outside.

"Forgive me for coming so early but I thought it best to speak in private," Bird began. Maureen nodded. "I don't think you understand the enormity of what you done last night." Maureen assured him that she didn't. "What made you stand? Why you done it?"

"I don't know," she said honestly. "I just thought

that something didn't feel right and before I knew it I was nominating myself."

"You got good instincts, girl. You're right. Richard Fischer's been running this farm with his own ideas for much too long. They even voted to extend term limits just so he could stay in power. With all due respect, I know he's a friend of yours but that Matthew Miller ain't nothin' but a puppet for that man. He's been moldin' him since the day he came."

"What's The Decision?"

"Oh, I think you already know. You're smart as a whip."

"Is it about sharing food, bringing it to the villages?"

Bird tapped his index finger to his nose twice. "You hit the nail right on the head," he said approvingly.

"Why doesn't Richard want to talk about it?"

"Why you even asking me, Girlie? You know. You know," Bird prodded gently.

"He doesn't want to expand the farm but why not? Why can't we share what we have here? Why can't we teach what we know to others?"

"He's a self-centered bastard, excuse my language. I haven't figured that one. He'll lose power? I dunno but we know where he stands. I'm with you. We oughter share it, 'specially since when know EZ Meal kills."

"They have my parents' research. They know how to fix EZ Meal."

"Then why the hell aren't we sharin' that information? Who told you that?"

"Richard."

"What an idjit. That just made The Decision easier. We got two steps. One, share the fix for EZ Meal first and two, try to reintegrate farming. It'll be harder than the back of God's head to do any of that with Miller in power and Richard pullin' the strings. If we want to change anything and I mean anything we got to get you elected Steward." A rooster crowed in the distance. It seemed to startle Bird. "We'll talk later. You be careful."

Maureen wasn't sure what he meant by that. She didn't think she was in danger but after what Bird had told her about Richard she wondered if she was. Richard Fischer was an intimidating man. He'd always put her on edge but he had been nothing but kind to her. She knew that was about to change.

She watched Bird limp off in the distance. No one else was out in the early morning chill. Maureen walked back inside to eat breakfast with her parents.

As promised, she spent the day canning with her mother and a large group of women. Maureen tried to pay attention and learn all she could about canning, as she had with bread baking the day before. Canning didn't hold her attention the way that baking bread had. She found her mind wandering, trying to decide what to do next, how to manage her candidacy and how to interact with Matthew. She thoughtlessly put her hand into a pot of boiling water to pull out a sanitized jar. She screamed out in pain. Her mother ran over to care for her burn. The rest of the morning she was assigned a chair in a corner with the understanding that she would watch and learn but stay out of the way. Maureen tried to pay attention to the fruits and vegetables and the pots of boiling water filled with glass jars. Despite her efforts of feigned interest, she was thankful that she had the entire morning to strategize.

At noon, Maureen and her mother headed home to eat lunch. On the farm, lunch was a simple meal usually consisting of a large piece of bread, some hard cheese and a piece or two of cured meat. Nicole tried to include fruit when they could. People working the fields, like her father, brought their lunch with them wrapped in a dishtowel so they didn't have to waste time walking home for lunch. Maureen learned that all the workers would sit in the shade and eat together. All through lunch, Nicole talked about how excited she was that Maureen loved canning the way she did. She was so happy to share it with her daughter. Maureen decided not to burst her bubble. She did ask that, since she couldn't help canning anymore that day on account of her burn, if she could spend some more time with the bread bakers. Her mother, clearly disappointed, said that would be fine. Maureen felt bad to disappoint her mother but she already knew that Ginger was an ally and needed to talk to her.

Maureen nearly ran to the large cabin, anticipating

the warm, sweet smell and the feel of the dough under her hands. She swung open the door without knocking expecting to find Ginger, Holly and Summer. She was startled to find Richard, Matthew, Davy and Pepper seated at the large table.

"Oh, I'm sorry. Excuse me. I thought Ginger would be baking bread in here," Maureen mumbled.

"The Potters are baking today. I don't know where Ginger is slotted," Pepper said.

"I'm so sorry," she mumbled again, walking backwards out of the door, certain that she'd stumbled upon a meeting about her. Matthew followed her outside.

"Can we talk?" he asked gruffly.

"'Course," Maureen said, glancing back at the cabin door, trying to imagine what Richard and Pepper were saying about her.

"Um, so, how you been?" Matthew began awkwardly.

"I've been better..." Maureen said.

"I thought we should talk about the election. Maybe we should plan a debate or something. We could share some ideas. I don't know," Matthew hung his head, embarrassed.

"Can we talk about something besides the election?"

"Yeah, sure."

"What brought you here? Did Richard?"

"No, I—I wanted to come. I knew that the way we were living wasn't right. I knew I had to get away."

"And being Richard's underling was part of the

plan?"

"No! Hey, Maureen. It's not like that at all. You just got here. You don't know anything." They stood for a moment, staring at the grass beneath their feet. It had only been a few years since they'd last seen each other but it felt like eons had passed.

"This isn't how I imagined it," Maureen said.

"It never is. Is that why you nominated yourself?"

"I don't know," Maureen answered honestly.

"What are you going to do? How are you — do you even know when the election is?"

"No," Maureen admitted, laughing a little. Matthew laughed too. His face softened and Maureen saw him relax for the first time. "Should you be consorting with the competition?" Maureen asked jokingly.

"You're no competition," Matthew returned with a friendly smile. Maureen felt a little stirring of old emotion for Matthew. Richard poked his head outside the door.

"Miller, we need you inside," he said.

Matthew's face hardened again. "Yes, sir," he replied. He glanced at Maureen as though to say something but walked inside the cabin silently.

Maureen stood outside the cabin trying to decide how to spend the afternoon. She was at a loss. A man walked by wearing overalls and a wide brimmed straw hat. Maureen had an idea.

"Excuse me. Is Anthony Plumber around?" Maureen asked the man.

"Yeah, he's the blacksmith in sector ten. You'll find him there," the man replied, tipping his hat to Maureen. "Good luck in the election," he added, winking at her.

"Thank you," Maureen replied and started walking towards sector ten to find Anthony.

Maureen walked through sector eight, passing log cabins set in clusters. Outside the schoolhouse she saw children breathlessly playing tag. She watched a group of women doing laundry in a creek, many of them wearing babies slung across their chests or backs. Maureen walked across the fields, watching the workers harvesting.

As the she entered sector nine she passed a group of men chopping wood. She saw a small group of teenagers carrying large containers of water to a storehouse. She passed stables and smelled the horses long before she could see them. She heard the sheep being rounded up by a dog. She saw cows, goats and chickens.

The landscape changed as Maureen neared sector ten. The fields closed in. Maureen thought she was in a forest until she realized fruit trees surrounded her. She was in an orchard. She couldn't identify most of the trees. They came in all sizes and shapes. Some looked more like bushes. She enjoyed the shade they provided. As she neared the center of sector ten it opened up again into a little square like sectors eight and nine did. She walked past the general store but it wasn't a store at all in the sense that Maureen understood it. It was where they stored supplies but no one had to pay for anything. They shared everything in common.

About a block away from the general store Maureen saw the blacksmith stall. It was hard to miss. Anthony was pulling something out of the fire with long metal tongs. He laid it on the anvil, holding it with the tongs and hammered at the glowing orange metal, sending sparks flying around him. Maureen walked up closer for a better look.

The noise was almost deafening. He was making horseshoes but Maureen didn't know enough about horses to know that. As usual, she was interested in anything new. She'd never thought about how metal was formed before. It wasn't as interesting as food preparation to her but it was pretty exciting to watch. After he finished shaping the horseshoe he put it aside to cool. He glanced up and saw Maureen.

"Maureen! I was hoping I'd see you soon." He pulled off his leather gloves and wiped his hands on the front of his filthy leather apron. He wiped the sweat off his forehead with his forearm, streaking ash across it. Maureen smiled. He stepped out of the stall.

"That's a pretty gutsy thing you did last night," Anthony said, smiling.

"I was hoping you could help me," Maureen started.

"As prodigal daughter you're pretty much a shoo-in. Anyone who's not Richard's protégé would probably win anyway." Maureen didn't know what "prodigal" meant but thought she understood anyway.

"I was hoping to talk with you about some farm

specifics. There's a lot I don't know. I was also hoping to talk some about The Decision. I thought you might help point me in the direction of some advisors."

"Whoa there. You're over-thinking this. You just have to be you. You're guaranteed to win the election."

"It's not just about winning. It's about doing a good job once I'm elected."

"Don't worry about it yet."

Maureen was upset. She wanted to like Anthony but every time she was convinced that she did, he managed to disappoint her.

"Anthony, I'm asking for help."

"You don't need it. You're going to win," he assured her, slapping her on the back with his massive hand.

"I was talking to," Maureen paused and decided not to mention Bird's name. "Another citizen and he had some serious concerns that I would like to address but I need some more background."

"Don't worry about it. Unless Richard rigs the election, you've got it in the bag."

Maureen walked away disappointed in Anthony. He wanted to be a revolutionary but he didn't have the heart for it. He didn't think things through. He'd probably never finished anything in his life. Maureen wondered what had happened to his collection. A part of her was almost certain he'd abandoned it in the warehouse in Harvest. She sighed heavily, mourning the loss of all those books, mourning the loss of Anthony as a friend.

CHAPTER 23

Within a week of arriving at the farm Maureen was on the duty roster. She was thankful to be baking with Summer, Ginger and Holly a couple days a week. She had grown close to them, especially Ginger. They spent hours discussing farm politics and helping her make plans. Summer, surprisingly, turned out to be a great ally. She quietly campaigned for Maureen. Maureen's campaign didn't have the pomp and circumstance of Matthew's but it had the people.

Her other main duty was caring for the preschool-age children, which irked her to no end. The children were sweet and she enjoyed being with them but it felt like a slap in the face. She had left that life only to have her CDT qualifications follow her to the farm. It didn't seem fair. She'd tried to protest the assignment and learned that once a ruling had been made it was difficult to appeal. It wasn't clear to Maureen how these assignments were made. She feared that Richard Fischer had found a way to harass her.

Most of all Maureen was surprised by how little she felt changed by being there. It was wonderful to have her parents back but after the initial shock she'd slipped right into the rhythm of life on the farm. The novelty of seeing her parents all the time wore off much more quickly than she would have imagined. She was already thinking of requesting her own living quarters soon. She'd thought that becoming a Foodie would solve all her problems, that this life would be better. She found it wasn't better, just different.

She was still forced to spend her days with three-year-olds. She was still unhappy with the people in charge. She still felt that she wasn't in control of what she did or who she spent time with. She still felt watched. It was beyond frustrating.

Maureen consoled herself by focusing on her campaign for Steward. She often met with Bird and Ginger. They gave her a history of the farm, teaching her all she would need to know to be the next Steward. They worked on their two-step plan to change the formula for EZ Meal and to reintegrate food. Maureen often told her parents goodnight and then disappeared for hours to meet with Bird and Ginger. Occasionally other people would join them in their meetings, sharing new information.

Maureen was surprised by how easily she took on a role of authority. Maureen couldn't decide what made this assignment different that all those class projects she hadn't wanted to lead. She finally decided it was the stakes. If her grade was at stake she would let someone else take the wheel but Maureen felt that this was about much more than the farm or even Harvest. Finally, all her hot-tempered rants had a place and maybe a purpose. She had a stirring in the pit of her stomach, that spurred her forward, that convinced her that this might be about the entire world in a way that she couldn't quite put into words yet.

For the most part, she stayed out of Matthew's way. They hadn't had much interaction. Maureen wasn't sure what she'd been expecting but she had thought they would at least be friends. It was painful to see Matthew and to feel awkward, to not know what to say around him, to not feel like she had permission to touch him. In fact, not touching him was the hardest part. Maureen felt herself swinging her arms a certain way or taking small, stumbling steps in order to not brush against Matthew. Richard kept him pretty busy. Maureen tried to get information on what they were planning but their entire operation was shrouded in secrecy.

In her spare time, which was scarce, Maureen tried to visit Travis whenever she could. She still felt responsible for him getting scrubbed. She wondered if she hadn't been nosing around if he would still be OK. She usually went to visit him during their day of rest, the one day a week that no one did any work. Maureen was accustomed to working seven days a week but she quickly adapted and learned to appreciate a day of rest. Although Maureen felt that she had many allies on the farm she didn't feel that she had many friends so she spent her free time with Travis.

Maureen walked quickly, her mind awash with thoughts of the election and her recent conversations with Bird and Ginger. Bird warned her that many of the older folks might be apt to vote for whomever Richard backed. Ginger tried to assure Bird that that was changing. It had erupted into a huge discussion about generational differences on the farm. Sometimes Maureen worried that there was too much she still didn't understand about life on the farm, that it was too different from life in Harvest for her to be a good Steward.

She spent most of her time working or meeting with folks and working out plans for when she was elected Steward. She wondered what she would do if she lost the election. How would she spend her time? What did everyone else do when they weren't working? Maureen had read in Harvest. It had been her only pleasure but there were very few books on the farm. Maureen was so lost in thought that she ran headlong into another person.

"Are you OK, Maureen?" It was Matthew. Maureen's heart sank.

"I'm fine," Maureen said, feeling the bump already forming on her forehead. She'd run straight into Matthew's arm. A large basket that he was carrying had obstructed his vision.

"I'm so sorry," Matthew said, setting down the basket and lifting his hand to her forehead. He hesitated a moment before brushing her forehead. "That'll leave a bump." Matthew made a face of regret.

"I'll be OK. You should watch where you're going."

"I was carrying a basket of potatoes. What's your excuse?" Maureen grew serious.

"Honestly, I was distracted thinking about the election. Are you worried? Do you think about it every waking minute?"

"No, not really. Richard takes care of the details."

"Oh, OK," Maureen said absently, sensing that the version of Matthew that she didn't care for was returning.

"I'm not worried about it because I know you'll win," Matthew said.

"You're just saying that."

"Word around the campfire is that you're gaining support with Richard's supporters. The question of my citizenship isn't helping matters."

"You can fight that. They voted that you could run."

Matthew cut her off. "Why would I fight it? I want you to win." Matthew put his hand to Maureen's forehead. "Do you want some ice?"

"No, I'm fine," Maureen winced at the slight pressure Matthew put on her forehead. "Maybe a little ice would be good."

"Do you know where the icehouse is?" Maureen shook her head no. "Let me drop off these potatoes and I'll take you." Matthew picked up the large basket. Maureen could tell how heavy it was by the way that Matthew picked it up. He carried it to a nearby storehouse. "The icehouse is this way," Matthew gestured to the left.

They walked in silence for a few moments.

"I never meant to be rivals," Matthew began. Maureen started to interrupt him. "Let me finish," Matthew said. "I never thought we'd be anything less than friends." Maureen heard an emphasis on "less." Did that mean that he might want to be more than friends?

"I'm so sorry about the state of things. Can we start over? Can we pretend I'm not running against you and that Richard decided I'm the next great hope of the farm? Clearly, you're the hope. Even though I've been here longer than you I can't help but think that you understand things I'm only beginning to grasp. You feel it in your bones. You were made to live here, made to do this and you know that."

"Not always. I still think there's so much I don't understand. How many other Foodie farms are there? How do we not know? Why aren't we in communication with them? Why haven't we tried to expand before? Matthew, I don't even know what lies beyond Harvest. Are there other villages just like it? Other farms? What does the world look like?"

"It's good that you ask those questions. We need someone to ask them." That wasn't the response that Maureen was hoping for. She wanted answers. Matthew sighed. "I don't know if anyone knows what the world looks like but I think you seem to know what it's supposed to look like."

Maureen rolled that thought around in her head. It seemed like a grandiose statement but running for Steward was kind of a grandiose idea itself. It meant that you thought you could do a better job than anyone else. It meant that you thought you had better ideas. Maureen thought about her life-long dissatisfaction and wondered if Matthew were right. Maybe that's where the feeling came from, knowing that it could be better and different and knowing that you could do something about it.

But when Maureen tried to imagine what that new world might be she faltered. She knew people lived on farms and shared food. She knew she baked bread. She knew that this world had books and art and leisure time. She thought that people might even have the opportunity to choose their own occupations. Maureen nodded. That all sounded right.

"What are you thinking about?" Matthew asked, noticing her nod.

"The new world," Maureen said, smiling. They had arrived at the icehouse. Matthew explained what happened to Basil, a large man who wore bright red suspenders. Basil cut off a chunk of ice, wrapped it in a cloth and handed it to Maureen.

"We're all rooting for ya," he said and winked. Maureen and Matthew walked back in the direction they had come. Maureen held the ice to her forehead. It was more difficult to think deep thoughts with the cold seeping into her brain. They returned to the scene of the head-bumping accident.

"Well, I should get back to the storehouse," Matthew said.

"Yeah, I'm on my way to see Travis." Maureen pointed in the direction she needed to walk.

"How's he doing?"

"Not good."

"Sorry. Take care of that bump." Matthew pivoted toward Maureen. He lifted his arm, hesitated and set it back down. "See ya," he said as he walked away.

"Bye," Maureen called after him. He was walking so quickly she wasn't sure he'd heard.

Maureen walked the rest of the way to the health lodge. She greeted Rosemary and asked how Travis was doing. Rosemary said that he was about the same but encouraged her to go sit with him. For weeks Travis had been the only patient. Maureen walked over to the sitting area where he usually spent most of his time. There was a pale blue fake leather couch, a few mismatched chairs and a metal coffee table. Nearby there stood a shelf full of books and games. Travis often spent his days working large jigsaw puzzles. Travis sat on the edge of the couch with puzzle pieces strewn about the coffee table in front of him. Maureen picked up the box top to see the horses running across the field.

Maureen greeted Travis and asked if she could help him with the puzzle. He eyed her suspiciously but agreed. Maureen sat next to him on the couch. Travis edged away from her slightly. Maureen stood and pulled a plastic and metal school chair up to the coffee table and sat across from him. Travis seemed to relax a bit. Maureen saw that he was assembling horse-colored pieces in a large pile so she started assembling grass-colored pieces in another area.

"How are you today?" Maureen asked.

"Fine," Travis said flatly. It was a short response but Maureen was glad that he was talking at all. He also seemed relatively calm. Some days he yelled and threw things because he didn't know where he was and he didn't recognize anyone. Maureen thought she'd probably yell and throw things too if she were that frightened.

They sat in silence working on the puzzle for at least an hour until Travis spoke. "Hey, I think you have one of my brown pieces. Right there, on the edge." He pointed to the piece.

"Oh, I think you're right. Here." Maureen passed him the piece.

"Thanks." Travis seemed satisfied when he got the final piece in the section he was working on. He even smiled a little. "Where am I, Maureen?" he asked without glancing up.

"You're in a hospital," she replied, pleased that he'd remembered her name.

"Am I sick?" Maureen thought for a second.

"Yes, we're trying to help you."

"What's wrong with me?"

"You don't remember things."

"But I do!" Travis insisted. "I remember lots of

things."

"Like what?"

"Yesterday I worked a different puzzle. It had cats on it." Rosemary told her he didn't have many memories at all but Maureen didn't want to believe it. In the back of her mind she'd really expected him to say something more substantial. "Also, I had a baby sister but she died," he said suddenly.

"You did!" Maureen encouraged. "Do you remember her name?"

"Annabelle," he said sadly. "She got sick and died. Am I going to die?"

"No, your illness isn't life-threatening."

"I know she was only a baby but I miss her sometimes." Maureen wasn't sure how to respond to that. She paused for a moment searching for something else to ask him about Annabelle.

"What did she look like?" she asked.

"Who?"

"Annabelle," Maureen encouraged. "Your sister," she added when Travis looked up from the puzzle with a blank expression.

"I don't have a sister," he said flatly. Maureen stood and left the room before Travis could see her tears. She ran into Rosemary on the way out and recounted the conversation. Rosemary said that it was very common for him to have moments of clarity like that. She said he'd never spoken of his sister before, though. She took out a spiral and made some notes. Maureen left the health lodge distraught.

She knew that Travis had been involved with the Foodies long before she visited him but she couldn't help feeling it was somehow her fault. She found herself walking in the direction of her parents' house. She walked about halfway there and then decided that wasn't where she wanted to be. She turned and walked the other way. She walked aimlessly heavy with worry, until it was time to be home for dinner.

After supper Maureen met with Bird and Ginger in Ginger's kitchen. They'd set up a command center there. Ginger's husband, Clove, and their two older children stayed in the other room. Clove insisted that he would like to help in any way that he could but he'd been relegated to child wrangler. Ginger wore their youngest child, Angus, against her chest in a sling. Little Angus was just a few weeks old.

They sat at the kitchen table, which was littered with correspondence, strategies and plans. They'd written out farm histories and timelines for Maureen. There were even a few family trees so Maureen could see how everyone was connected. They had piles of suggestions that Ginger had requested from people. It was heartening that most of the suggestions aligned with their plans. Maureen stared at a page that detailed the election rules. She was surprised that an agrarian society would have so many written documents. She had to remind herself that most of these people's ancestors had lived in Harvest and the surrounding areas. None of these families had been farmers for very long.

They exchanged pleasantries for a few minutes.

Then Maureen asked, wearily, "How are the contacts going?"

"Not great," Ginger replied. "We just don't have the infrastructure. I was able to contact Linden over in the North Territory. He said he'd get word of our plans to Margarita over near Black Mountain. Word is moving very slowly. I'm not sure how we'll be able to give the go-ahead when it's time. The farms are so loosely connected."

"But they're connected. That's what matters. We can make this work," Maureen replied, trying to convince herself. "What was their reaction?"

"Good. Favorable. Linden said we might have some more trouble with the coastal regions but the North Territory and Black Mountain are with us," Ginger replied. Maureen exhaled as though she'd been holding her breath waiting for the response.

"Good," Maureen said.

"You all right, Girlie?" Bird asked.

"I'm fine. I've just...got a lot on my mind," Maureen replied attempting a smile.

"The pressure gettin' to ya?" Bird asked.

"Maybe a little." Maureen felt a tear that she hadn't known was there fall down her cheek. Ginger scooted her chair closer and pulled her into a tight hug with Angus between them.

"If anyone can do this, it's you," she said with more certainty than Maureen felt. Maureen blinked away any future tears. She turned to Bird, "How is the armory going?"

CHAPTER 24

Maureen sat with Clementine crying in her lap. Maureen often sat with Clementine crying in her lap. She sighed heavily, trying to will the election to come sooner. When she was elected Steward her placement on the duty roster would change significantly. She was already trying to formulate a new plan for assigning future jobs. She wasn't the only one unfulfilled by her work assignments. Maureen knew that someone had to muck out stalls and watch the preschoolers but there had to be a better way to make assignments.

Maureen's thoughts wandered to Travis. Travis's treatment had been progressing poorly. Recently, Rosemary had told Maureen that he may never fully recover. Maureen had wept all night. In the same conversation, Rosemary had asked her not to come visit as often. Maureen bounced Clementine and tried to push away thoughts of Travis. She couldn't accomplish anything feeling guilty about Travis all the time.

Rosemary came running into the nursery.

"Maureen! Travis is asking for you!" Rosemary was exultant, grinning from ear to ear. Maureen looked at Cooper, one of the other nursery workers.

"What are you waiting for? Go see him! I can call Anise to come help me," Cooper said.

"Are you sure? Should I wait until she gets here?"

"Just go," Cooper urged. He took Clementine out of Maureen's arms. Clementine immediately stopped crying as though all of Maureen's insecurities, thoughts and fears had been upsetting her. Maureen was too occupied with thoughts of Travis to even notice. She left with Rosemary.

"How is he? What's happened?" Maureen asked.

"This morning he woke up and asked where you were," Rosemary said, out of breath. "He asked, 'Where's Maureen?' like you'd been there when he went to sleep. I decided to come and get you since he seemed so lucid."

"I'm glad you did. I hope seeing me is helpful." Rosemary smiled at her nervously. Maureen got the feeling that she was leaving something out. Before she had the opportunity to say anything else they arrived at the health lodge and Rosemary showed her in.

Once, when Maureen had come to see him he'd been so absorbed in the puzzle he'd never acknowledged her presence. Today he jumped up off the couch.

"Maureen!" he called, his face lighting up. He embraced her tightly. "I was so worried when I woke up

223

and you weren't here. I thought that maybe..." Travis glanced behind Maureen to see Rosemary. He pointed at her. "Can we ask her to leave?" Maureen looked back at Rosemary.

"I can leave you two alone," Rosemary said, leaving the room and closing the door behind her.

"What is it?" Maureen asked, worried that Rosemary had done something to him without being able to imagine what it could possibly be.

"I thought Sam got to you, too," Travis said, sitting back down on the couch. He patted the cushion next to him for Maureen to sit. Maureen sat.

"What about Sam?" she asked, absently. She was used to Travis not being coherent.

"I was afraid that he got you, too."

"Got me?" Maureen started sorting the edge puzzle pieces. Travis grew serious again.

"Yeah, who do you think did this to me?" Maureen dropped the puzzle pieces in her hand. She turned slowly to look at Travis.

"What?" She couldn't find the words for the question starting to form in her mind.

"Your brother, Sam. He's the one who scrubbed me."

"Travis, it's been a really hard couple of months for you. This is the first time you've recognized me. I don't think you know what you're saying..." Travis griped Maureen by her arms and stared into her eyes with his soul-searching gaze.

"Maureen Baker, your brother, Sam Baker, my

best friend for most of my life, is the person who scrubbed me. I know this. I remember this. I remember everything."

Maureen stood up suddenly. "But that can't be. Maybe it was someone who looked like Sam and your brain is just filling in the blanks with Sam. I mean he couldn't. There's no way..."

"Why do you think he never wanted to move? Why do you think he discouraged you searching for the Foodies? Why do you think he never tried to avenge your parents? He knew—maybe not everything but he knew a lot and in order to keep him quiet..."

"No. It's not true. There's no way Sam could do that."

"He works for them. He works for Jasper security."

"No he doesn't!" Maureen yelled. "I don't believe you!"

"That day I missed our meeting I was with Sam. I'd told him too much. Sam knew how I communicated with the Foodies. I saw the sign, a chalk mark on the stop sign at Elm and Oak. So I went to the usual location at the usual time but I found Sam. He was in tears when I got there. He told me I shouldn't have told him so much. He said it was my fault and the whole time," Travis paused, wincing, "the whole time that he was...scrubbing he apologized. I'll never forget it. I hadn't seen him cry since he was seven and got stung by that wasp." Maureen sat down slowly. It was difficult to admit to herself but she'd known. She didn't know how to admit that her own brother was the enemy.

"I am, so sorry. I can't begin," Maureen said.

Travis interrupted her, "You don't need to. I just had to tell you. Your safety was my first thought since that was the last thing I remembered. Rosemary tried to catch me up but it wasn't making a lot of sense. You're running for Steward of the farm?" Travis smiled.

"Yeah."

"I'll vote for you."

Maureen smiled. She thought for a moment. "Now what?" Maureen asked.

"What do you mean?"

"What do we do about Sam?"

"We don't do anything. He's made his choices. We've made ours."

They worked on the puzzle in silence for a few moments, both of them slowly becoming aquatinted with the new reality.

"Are they going to put you on the duty roster or are you supposed to just keep working on puzzles? Not that I'm implying that you're not skilled at puzzles and that your contribution of assembling puzzles isn't important," Maureen said.

"I happen to be the very best puzzler on the farm, thank you very much. Rosemary said they need to observe me for a couple more days. I think she's afraid I'll wake up tomorrow and not be able to remember anything. Is there anything else I need to tell you while I can still remember?" Travis searched Maureen, trying to remember and trying to see what other information she lacked. Maureen shook her head.

"I'm really sorry about Sam," Travis said as Maureen stood to leave.

"Not as sorry as I am." Maureen walked out of the health lodge in a daze. She didn't go back to the nursery. For all Anise knew she might be there all day. She had a hall pass and she intended to use it. Maureen had to reorient. She had to rework everything she thought she knew all over again. It had been an all too familiar experience in the past few months. It could take her all day to remember that her brother worked for Jasper security and had hurt his best friend. It could take her a lifetime to reconcile that fact with the man she'd known.

CHAPTER 25

Maureen found herself wandering. She didn't have a destination in mind but she couldn't sit still with her thoughts and she didn't want to talk to anyone. If she continued walking her thoughts almost couldn't catch up with her. She only needed to remain one step ahead to keep from being engulfed.

One day, Dilly Mason had shown her where the children often went to play. There was a heavily wooded area out behind one of the storehouses. Hidden in the woods were a tree house and a swing. The tree house was built out of scrap wood. It had a rope ladder that the older children pulled up to keep the little ones out. It had a roof so many of the children stored their treasures up there. Adults were not allowed. Some days it was a castle. Other times it was a pirate ship. Whatever game they were playing usually seemed to require squealing.

Maureen had a vague idea of swinging in the swing for a few hours. She thought that maybe if she swung high enough everything would be all right, the broken pieces would resettle into something that made sense, like Travis's puzzles. She just had to put the pieces together correctly. She often went to the swing alone to think, while the children were in school or late at night. She'd come to love the night, now that she no longer had any reason to fear it.

She turned behind the storehouse and started walking into the woods before she noticed movement. She was almost upon the swing before she stopped. Matthew was swinging in the swing. He didn't sense her presence. He was swinging with a relaxed expression on his face. He looked a little silly, such a large man swinging on the child-sized swing. Maureen recognized him. It was her friend from high school Matthew Miller. Whatever life or Richard Fischer had done to him had no power over him now. Maureen contemplated leaving the clearing. She felt like she was trespassing and didn't want to disturb him. She started to back away slowly but she stepped on a twig and startled Matthew out of his reverie. He dug his foot into the ground to stop the swing. "Who's there?" he called, nervously. Richard probably didn't approve of adults swinging on swings.

"It's just me," Maureen smiled, walking towards him.

"Maureen." Matthew smiled back. "Now you know my secret."

"And you know mine. I come here all the time." Matthew stood and gestured towards the seat.

Maureen waved her hand. "No, that's OK. You were here first." She walked closer to the swing.

"Really, have a seat. I'll push you,"

"OK," Maureen accepted. She sat in the swing and Matthew grasped the wooden seat in his hands, pulled it back and let it go. Maureen swung forward. When she returned to him Matthew gently pushed her on the small of her back. Matthew pushed her in silence for a few minutes. Maureen felt the breeze in her hair. When she swung forward she closed her eyes and everything dropped away.

"So what do you think about all this? Should I just concede the election to you right now?" Matthew asked.

Maureen opened her eyes. "I don't know. It's still anybody's game."

"Come on, you know that's not true. The election's just for show at this point, isn't it?" Matthew said without any bitterness.

"Are you going to be all right if I win?"

"All right? It'll be a relief. I know I can't explain it to you now but Richard really is a good man. He's just trying to do what he thinks is right for the farm. But maybe what used to be right isn't anymore."

"I don't doubt that he thinks he's doing what's right for Richard Fischer. I'm more concerned about everybody else."

"And I think we need that," Matthew replied earnestly. He paused, "I think you're brilliant. I think whatever you've been cooking up with Bird and Ginger will be..."

"You think I'm brilliant?" Maureen interrupted

skeptically.

"Of course, I always have."

"Always?"

"Always. Hey, I've been meaning to tell you I'm sorry about..."

"Me too. Don't worry about it. We're good now, right?"

"Right." Matthew pushed Maureen on the swing. After months of trying to not touch she was acutely aware of his hand on her back. There was nothing suggestive or sexual about it, the palm of his hand, pressing her back but she couldn't help feeling that the palm of his hand was communicating the secrets of the universe to her, if only she could understand them.

As Maureen swung back Matthew grabbed the swing's ropes and Maureen came to a sudden halt. She was able to put out a foot to keep from falling forward. Matthew walked in front of her.

"We're not good, are we? We're still not all right. Maybe we are. I don't know," he said.

"I think we're fine."

"Right, fine but not good, not great. I think we could be great. In fact, I think we should be great. Because you're brilliant and I've always thought you're the most beautiful girl and I—I think I've loved you since I was fourteen. I want to be more than fine with you." Matthew took a deep breath and said, "I want to be more than friends with you and have kids with you and grow old with you." He paused and swallowed hard. "I'm sorry, that was stupid."

Maureen interrupted him by standing and grabbing him by the back of the neck. Matthew obliged by leaning down to kiss her. It was every high school fantasy come true. Only this time they were adults so there wasn't too much slobber and their teeth didn't knock. It was the fairy tale kiss she'd always dreamed of. Maureen and Matthew embraced.

"Maybe we should try dating before the whole kid thing," Maureen joked.

"If that's what you want. I guess we could give it a shot first." Matthew smiled.

Maureen pushed Matthew away playfully. "Does this change the election at all? Is Richard going to kill you?"

"The election will be fine. You'll win, as you should and I don't care what Richard thinks anymore." Matthew leaned in to kiss Maureen again.

After they parted Maureen said, "We should probably keep this quiet for a couple days so it doesn't appear to be an impropriety."

"Of course. I agree. But a day or two after the election I'm going to shout from the rooftops that you're my girl."

"*Your* girl?"

"Yeah, *my* girl." Matthew grabbed her by the waist and kissed her again. For the first time they both noticed how close it was to dusk.

"I've got to get home for dinner. My parents are going to wonder where I am." Her own words jolted her back to reality. She'd completely forgotten about the morning's events. "I have some things to tell you but not now. Remind me later," she said as she kissed him one last time and ran off towards her parents' cabin. Maureen made it through the door just as her father was setting the table.

"We were about to send out a search party. Where-e've you been?" Bill asked. "We saw Cooper a little while ago and he said that Travis was asking for you and that he hadn't seen you since then."

"Travis is doing great. He remembers everything. Rosemary is worried that it's only temporary but I think he's back," Maureen replied, washing her hands in the kitchen sink.

"Oh, that's so wonderful," Nicole exclaimed.

"Well, some of what he remembers isn't wonder-ful..."

"Like what, Pumpkin?" Bill asked, ruffling her hair as they sat at the table. Nicole filled their bowls with chicken potpie.

"I'm afraid to ask because I think I already know the answer. Did you know that Sam works for Jasper security?" Maureen said. Nicole and Bill exchanged a serious look.

"Yes," Bill responded.

"For the love of—why didn't you tell me?" Maureen was exasperated. "Do you not trust me? Why do you insist on treating me like a child? I can handle the truth."

"You're our child and we're never going to stop

trying to protect you. We weren't sure if you'd ever find out and we didn't want to tarnish your brother's memory," Nicole explained.

"Are you saying you thought Travis would never recover?"

"We hoped he would but we knew it was possible he might not. We also weren't positive that it was your brother who'd scrubbed him. I guess now we know," Bill said.

"I can't believe that after everything you're still keeping things from me. What else do you need to tell me? Let's just get it all out on the table now."

"Pumpkin, I promise there's nothing else. We just didn't see the need to tell you something that would only hurt you," Bill said.

"It's actually something that might hurt us all. If Sam knows everything that Travis knows it means they know where we are. They could come get us at any time," Maureen said.

Nicole waved her hand. "They've always known. That's not a concern."

"What do you mean?"

"They know where we are. They leave us alone as long as we don't harass people in Harvest," Bill said casually.

"But they threaten us. Aren't you afraid that they'll make good one day?"

"Not really. If it was going to happen it would have happened years ago," Nicole said.

"For a while, our recruitment numbers were high.

People were defecting and joining us left and right. If they were going to get upset with us it would have been then," Bill said.

"So they know we're a joke and we're not a threat at all? They don't care what we do because it only affects us?" Maureen said frustrated by this entire situation and even more determined to move out of her parents' cabin. She understood their point of view but that didn't mean she had to agree with it.

"Are you worried about the election tomorrow?" Nicole asked.

"Mom, this isn't about the election. I just don't understand...you people."

"*Your* people. We're *your* people. You're one of us," Nicole insisted.

"Sometimes. I know I am when I'm kneading bread. I know it's something I was born to do. It makes my heart sing. I'm a baker through and through," Maureen replied dreamily. She furrowed her brow, "But I can't believe the way you manage things. I don't get your weird relationship with Jasper Industries. I don't get how you could lie to your own children for so long. I don't get it. Help me understand. Give me the full history. I've learned a lot in the past few months but I know there's more you're keeping from me."

"It's not like that," Nicole said.

"You're free to return to Harvest whenever you like," Bill said angrily.

"Dad! That's not what I'm saying at all! I just want

to understand. That's all I'm asking," Maureen said.

"Just tell her," Nicole said quietly.

Bill turned to her. "Are you sure? With the election tomorrow? Maybe..."

"Tell her," Nicole insisted.

"I don't think," Bill began.

Nicole interrupted him, "I'm glad that you're running for Steward and I'm glad that you're asking these questions. They sound different when someone else asks them out loud. I'm ashamed at the way some things have been handled. I am so thankful that you're here and I think that we need you." Nicole took a deep breath. "Bird had a vision many years ago."

"Nicole!" Bill shot her a warning look.

"She needs to know! When you were a baby, Bird had a vision that you would lead us. That's partly why people treat you the way they do." Nicole's face crumpled and her voice grew higher as she started to cry, "That's why we've been expecting you. That's why we knew you would come."

"But Mom, how could he know that? How could anyone?"

"He couldn't. It was a horrible burden to put on a child so we didn't tell you. Some people are voting for you for purely superstitious reasons," Bill said.

Nicole shot Bill an admonishing look. "Sweetie, did you keep the cookbook?" she asked.

"Of course."

Nicole smiled through her tears. "I knew."

They sat in silence, the air heavy with words unspoken. Maureen felt a crushing weight on her chest, like someone was sitting on it. Her vision blurred. She tried to focus and failed. Maureen stood suddenly and became dizzy. She clutched the edge of the table to keep from falling.

"I'm meeting with Ginger and Bird. I've got to go."

Maureen walked slowly to Ginger's cabin for their final meeting before the election. They still had some important details to hash out but Maureen realized she just didn't have the energy for it. So now she wasn't just the prodigal daughter but the fulfillment of a prophecy? It was too much to take. When she arrived at the house Ginger saw the exhaustion on her face, shooed her away and told her to get some sleep.

CHAPTER 26

Election Day arrived before the dawn. Maureen lay awake all night. She knew her candidacy was the right choice. She'd been meeting with Bird and Ginger for months. The plan felt solid. It would be difficult but it felt right and now Maureen understood the reason why she felt like she had to be the one to implement it. Maureen had never really thought much about destiny or fate before. It didn't make sense to think about it when you lived a little, solitary life. The idea that her life was more than simply a series of events but a destiny, culminating in something significant gave Maureen renewed focus and confidence.

As Maureen lay in bed in the loft wearing a soft cotton nightgown she couldn't help but think that something beyond herself had brought her there. All those people knowing who she was, all those questions she'd had, all the people she'd met had led her here. And something beyond herself had encouraged her to run for Steward. Maureen still didn't have a name for that feeling. She hadn't spoken to anyone about it but it almost felt as though someone had called her name and she'd simply stood up. Here, I'm here. It was confusing to think about but the inclusion of Bird's vision filled in some of the missing pieces. For the first time in her entire life, Maureen felt she was seeing the entire picture splayed out in front of her and it was beautiful.

She thought about the kiss she shared with Matthew at the swing. Finally, that felt right too. It had been so heartbreaking to not feel that Matthew was a friend. She was thrilled yet cautious about their new relationship. It was what she'd wanted since she was fourteen. It would be difficult for anything to live up to those kinds of expectations, to survive under that kind of pressure.

Pressure. Maureen's thoughts wandered back to the election. The pressure had just begun. If this is what it felt like before the election Maureen couldn't imagine the pressure of being in charge. She tried to swallow the lump forming in her throat but it seemed to stick. Would their plan really work? Did they really have the support they thought they did? Ginger had assured her that Sage from the south country and Laurel from Ponil River were with them too. The group grew every day. Every day another farm joined them. Every day another farm offered resources: food, land, vehicles, and weapons. Maureen cringed thinking about the weapons. She hoped they wouldn't have to use them but knew it was a fantasy. Jasper Industries would hold tight to its control of humanity.

Maureen thought about Travis. She cheered a bit, remembering his full recovery. The heaviness left her chest for a moment. She hoped that he was completely back, even if that meant that Sam was gone. The heaviness returned to weigh down on her heart. Maureen pushed the thought of Sam out of her head. It hurt too much to think of her brother causing anyone harm, let alone his best friend.

Maureen was growing antsy. She made up her bed and changed out of her cotton nightgown into a blue gingham knee length dress. She walked down the loft ladder. It was still dark outside but she couldn't lay there anymore. She snuck out of the house knowing exactly where she was going.

It was calming to be awake and outside before anyone else. The world felt clean and simple. A cool breeze rustled her hair and she was glad that she didn't have a ponytail holder to tame it. For a moment she just stared up at the stars, thinking about what they'd seen, hoping they'd share their secrets with her. She felt certain that the stars held the answers if she could only learn their language. The full moon was so bright she didn't need a lantern.

About fifteen minutes later she arrived at the swing in the woods to find Matthew swinging alone. He smiled and approached her without a word. It was as though they'd planned a clandestine meeting in the woods all along. They embraced and kissed. Then they both lay down in the little clearing, cuddling up next to one another in the cool early morning. They looked up at the sky. Neither of them spoke.

Maureen tried to clear her mind of every thought, tried to rid it of clutter. She laid with her head on Matthews chest. She grasped his hand and Matthew squeezed her hand. Maureen wondered if there were other people in other lands making similar decisions. What was life like on that star? Were they fighting corporations that were set up to do good but that had lost their center? Wasn't that an essential problem, losing your center, forgetting why?

EZ Meal had saved lives but Jasper Industries had grown out of control and stopped progress toward growing food again. Not sharing meals with people had led to...Maureen wasn't even sure what since she'd only just recovered it but it felt important. It felt like a part of her had been missing, a part she never knew she lacked. She felt connected. She no longer felt adrift. She knew her place. For the first time in her life she felt she had people and the thought made her heart swell so much she thought it might burst. She wanted to help other people see what she saw and if home baked bread was the answer she wanted to bake for the rest of her life.

Lying out in the clearing in the cool, dark early morning, holding Matthew's hand everything felt so simple. It was clear what had to happen. It wasn't a question. It was an imperative. After what felt like a few minutes but was surely at least an hour, Maureen sat up. She kissed Matthew again, stood and walked away, all without exchanging a single word. She knew he understood.

As she walked she combed her fingers through her hair, removing twigs and leaves. She brushed off the back of her dress and then returned to raking her fingers through her hair. It looked like she'd rolled around out there for the amount of debris she found in her hair. The sky began to brighten and the sun had nearly risen by the time she arrived home.

She joined her parents at the breakfast table. They didn't ask where she had been. Maureen felt calm and collected. Her parents were clearly nervous for her. She was grateful that they didn't say anything to ruin her mood. After they finished eating, her mother pulled a leaf out of her hair but thankfully didn't say anything.

No one worked on Election Day. It was a huge celebration with dancing and, of course, food. No matter who won the election the idea was that everyone left in good spirits. Everyone looked forward to the big party afterward. They'd been preparing food for days. They'd even slaughtered a few goats, which they only did for special occasions. It was going to be a feast.

Maureen walked over to the pavilion early. Ginger and baby Angus were already there. Ginger was talking to Elliott Potter, one of the election officials, a tall thin man who wore a bowler hat. Ginger smiled broadly when Maureen approached.

"There she is now, Madame Steward! That's not what we call you, is it?" Ginger smiled again. "It's going to be a lovely day." Angus cooed in seeming agreement. "We've only got an hour or so until people start showing up. Is there anything you need me to do?"

"No, I just want to sit and be quiet. And maybe not talk to anyone," Maureen said.

"Done," Ginger said, spreading out her hands and walking away. Maureen sat on one of the benches by the podium at the front of the pavilion. She tried to regain the feeling she had the night before but it was impossible in the sun. She couldn't empty her mind with sweat dripping down her back. The autumn breeze did nothing to cool her. She thought about discarding her white cardigan but decided to leave it on. Removing it wouldn't stop her from sweating.

Quickly people started to file into the pavilion. People greeted Maureen and shook her hand and wished her luck. Children ran around, acting wilder than usual. Everyone could feel the electricity in the air. Matthew gazed at Maureen from across the pavilion. Even though twenty people were trying to talk to her at once she was only aware of Matthew.

Once everyone had arrived, Elliott Potter began to explain the voting procedure. Maureen's mind was racing but she remembered the procedure from Bird and Ginger's lessons. Every person over the age of thirteen was given a dry bean. There were two large metal cans, clearly labeled, one for Matthew and one for Maureen. They were put in a storehouse and everyone would walk in, one at a time, and place their bean in one of the cans. Elliott Potter and Flor would sit at a table and watch that no one tampered with the beans and only they would know how everyone voted, although they claimed they didn't remember. After the last vote had been cast, Elliott Potter would assemble the rest of the election committee. Elliott, Flor, Ivy and Narciso counted the beans to tally the results. The results would be announced at the dance, which people joined once they'd cast their vote.

Elliott, Flor, Ivy and Narciso walked up and down the rows of benches handing out beans, keeping track of who received them and how many they passed out. Finally they made their way up to the front of the pavilion and handed beans to Matthew and his advisors: Richard, Pepper and Davy and to Maureen and hers: Bird and Ginger. Finally, Elliott announced that voting had begun and asked Maureen and Matthew to cast their ballots first. Maureen followed Elliott into the storehouse. She blinked, giving her eyes a moment to adjust to the darkness in the storehouse after being out in the bright sunlight. Sacks of grains were piled high behind a little table with two chairs. Elliott and Flor sat in their places. Two metal cans stood on the little table; one said Matthew Miller, the other said Maureen Baker. Flor griped a clipboard in one hand and a pencil in the other. "Maureen Baker," she said under her breath as she put a check mark by Maureen's name.

Maureen stood for a long moment staring at the metal cans. Were these the cans they always used or had these cans recently held food items? Maureen felt odd voting for herself but then she thought of Richard's influence on Matthew. She dropped her bean into the can marked Maureen Baker. For perhaps the first time, Maureen thought she saw a little smile on Flor's serious face. Maureen walked out of the storehouse. As she walked out she passed Matthew walking in. He squeezed her hand as she brushed past him. Maureen blushed, wondering if anyone had seen.

Maureen headed towards another large covered pavilion constructed very much like the other with a metal roof, however this pavilion didn't have rows of benches and it had a carefully leveled floor covered with wood planks for dancing. After she and Matthew voted, the musicians would be close behind so they could get the party started. Maureen felt a little lost to be the first person at the dance pavilion. Arriving before the musicians felt like arriving while the host was still getting dressed. Surrounding the edges of the pavilion were picnic tables and benches. Other tables were filled with food. Maureen walked by the food tables, identifying potato salad, green beans, cheese, fresh bread, apple pies, cookies, and cakes. It was a feast that Maureen wouldn't have been able to imagine a few months ago. The dishes started to blur together. Maureen realized she was no longer registering what she was seeing.

Even though Maureen was excited for the celebration and she was excited to be Steward the two events seemed incongruous in her mind. Being Steward would probably be the most difficult thing she'd ever done. Sitting in a dark room alone, contemplating the consequences seemed more appropriate than a party.

Matthew flashed her a huge grin as he came to join her on one of the benches surrounding the pavilion. Shortly after, the band followed and started to play. Maureen had only recently become acquainted with bluegrass music. She especially loved the sound of the banjo and was delighted by the makeshift instruments: the washboard, the jug, and the spoons. She loved the idea that utilitarian objects could make music. Soon the dance floor was filled with skirts whirling about the dance floor like flags in the wind. Children chased one another, squealing with glee or dancing around their parents. Other sat at the tables watching the dancers and chatting with friends.

Maureen watched as some men grilled goats on huge open grills. The smell of the cooking meat filled the air and mingled with the smell of sweets from the other tables. Wilford Brewer had brewed beer for the occasion. He handed out mugs of beer, laughing loudly and clanking glasses with anyone nearby. Children drank glasses of lemonade. Colorful fabric bunting flapped in the cool Autumn breeze.

Matthew stood and held out his hand to Maureen. She took it, not knowing what to expect. Matthew led her to the dance floor and began swinging her around just like everyone else. For a brief moment Maureen was worried she would smash into another dancer or end up on the floor. She quickly learned that Matthew was a talented dancer and that if she trusted him and followed him she could fly around the dance floor. Maureen had never been happier in her life.

CHAPTER 27

It took a few minutes for Maureen to realize what was happening. A man ran up to the pavilion but that didn't seem odd. Some adults were playing with the children and chasing them around making animal noises. No one seemed to notice this man until Richard approached him. Richard appeared angry and tried to keep the man away from the pavilion. The crowd was so loud that no one heard the exchange between them. Finally, Richard whistled loudly placing two fingers in his mouth; it was a skill that everyone on the farm had. Children learned the skill at a young age. It signaled danger.

Immediately the music stopped. The dancers froze in mid-air. No one said a word. Richard moved towards the revelers with the man close behind him. The man looked familiar but a black eye, a split lip and a large, swollen bruise on his right cheek distorted his face. Finally, Maureen placed him: Herman.

Richard stood near the edge of the pavilion, in the midst of everything. It was so silent Maureen swore she could hear every heard pounding. Richard glanced around gravely, with a pained expression on his face before speaking.

"Herman is here to give us some information. He is risking his life being here, both because Jasper Industries might kill him and because we might. We need to acknowledge this risk." He paused for a moment to let the enormity of what he'd said permeate the air. "Herman, tell them what you told me," Richard ordered.

"Jim Jasper, James Jasper the third and his father, James Jasper, Jr. are both dead."

A gasp traveled through the group.

"Are you sure James Jr. was still alive? He must have been ancient," someone called out.

"We're sure. My sources say that they both died in a lab accident. Junior was trying to come up with a fix for EZ Meal," Herman replied. Eyes turned to Maureen's parents. Maureen wondered if people were thinking this could have been prevented if they'd shared their knowledge. It was what she was thinking.

"Are you sure they both died?" Maureen found herself saying. She knew Richard was glaring at her. "My parents died in a lab accident, too," she turned to her frightened parents. A few people giggled nervously. Others nodded.

"That's a good point," Herman agreed. "But I was nearby. I saw the bodies. What this means is Jimmy, James Jasper the fourth is in charge."

"That's a good thing, right?" Maureen asked, remembering her exchange with him.

"No, it's not," Richard, replied stonily.

"Richard's right," Herman said. "He's not taking their deaths well, especially Junior's. He was particularly close to him. He thinks that trying to find a solution to the EZ Meal problem caused their deaths. My intel says that he's planning to take it out on the Foodies."

"That doesn't make sense. It's not our fault," Maureen interjected.

"It doesn't have to make sense to be a real threat," Richard said.

Maureen instantly felt naive. "What does this all mean for us?" Maureen asked.

"It means they're planning a raid on sectors eight through twelve, at the very least." Herman turned to Richard. "What's your firepower like these days?"

"Not great. We've been working on," Richard began.

"We've got the backing of every Foodie farm from here to the coast. Black Mountain and the East recently joined us too," Maureen interrupted him. The expression on Richard's face told her he was surprised and impressed. "They're with us if we have time to give them the go-ahead," Maureen continued.

"We may not have time. We need to tell them to be on alert. If we're in danger, everyone is," Richard said.

In the midst of the confusion of Herman's arrival and his subsequent news no one had noticed the absence of Ivy, Elliott, Narciso and Flor. They appeared at the storehouse door, Flor holding her official-looking clipboard. They immediately knew that something was wrong. Everyone stood in silence, their eyes traveling between Herman, Richard and Maureen.

Flor broke the silence, "We have the election results," she said loudly. Every head turned to look at the speaker at the same time. Maureen imagined she heard a whoosh sound. "Our new Steward is Maureen Baker." Maureen felt every eye on her.

CHAPTER 28

They sent word out to every Foodie farm they'd managed to make contact with and asked them to spread the news further if possible. They started working on their weapon stores with increased urgency. They tried to build up their food stores and jarred as much water as possible. They discussed what to do with children and pregnant women, where they would be safest. It was decided that they would be safer hiding in the woods. An evacuation plan was made.

Maureen was all nerves. She was terrified of what was going to happen. She'd never shot a gun until a few weeks ago when Bird insisted she needed to learn. Everyone looked to her for answers. She tried her best to answer what she could. Bird and Ginger continued to be essential advisers. Maureen started to realize that everyone seemed calmer and more focused after they spoke with her. Maybe this was exactly where she was supposed to be.

Herman stayed on the farm, although people remained suspicious of him. Some people worried that he would run back to Jasper Industries and report what they were planning. He repeatedly claimed he would do no such thing. He was a man without a country. He had nowhere to go. Maureen remembered that feeling and pitied him but not enough to spend any time with him outside meetings.

Maureen walked towards a cabin for a meeting with a group of teenagers who had agreed to care for the children. They were to tie up some of the loose ends for the evacuation, which was to occur the next day. Herman walked directly up to Maureen.

"I never meant for any of this to happen," he said pleadingly. He sounded so pathetic, so wounded. Maureen believed him.

"I know," she responded and continued on to her meeting.

"It wasn't supposed to be like this!" Maureen stopped walking and turned to face him. "I had no choice. They would have killed both of us if I hadn't done what I did."

"I know."

"Do you forgive me?"

"No. Maybe." She took a breath. "I don't know. I don't know if I'd be here if I hadn't met you. And I know this is where I need to be." They stood in silence.

"Does he still call you Lamb?"

"No." Maureen turned on her heels and went to her meeting.

They came in the dead of night. It was the day the children's' evacuation was scheduled and two days before they would have been as prepared as possible. Many farms remained to be contacted. There was still jarring to be done and resources to be gathered. They simply weren't ready. The Foodies slept fitfully in their beds, making plans, worrying.

Maureen hadn't slept more than a few hours since Herman's arrival. She spent her nights swinging in the swing in the woods. Most nights Matthew joined her. They made love like it might be the last time. Then they'd lay together in the leaves sometimes talking but usually just trying to remember to breathe amid the imminent confrontation.

Lying in the cool dark night, she'd try to remember what they were forgetting. She always felt like they were forgetting something important. She knew that it would happen too soon, that they wouldn't be fully ready. She knew the children should have left the moment Herman arrived but it had been impossible. They needed food and water. They needed people to go with them. They needed a plan. And plans take time. Time that they didn't have.

While she spent most her of time thinking about practical matters, problems that needed solutions at that very moment, she also spent some time thinking about the future. Most people had a hard time seeing past the raid. Since Herman's arrival the preparations for the raid were at the front of everyone's mind.

People accepted that there would be some causalities from the raid but Maureen was preparing for the worst, mentally and physically. She was also preparing for the future beyond the raid. Maureen thought that if she were to die in the raid, she needed her life to count for something.

And so, while everyone else was collecting weapons and packaging food, Maureen got a message to Margarita near Black Mountain. She gave explicit instructions for Black Mountain to not enter the fighting. She had other plans for them. She expected Margarita to resist, to disagree with her. Margarita's letter had said, "You understand the struggle better than anyone. Thank you for this most important mission." Maureen didn't know if it would work but she knew it was worth trying.

From the clearing in the woods, Maureen heard a scrambling noise. It reminded her of the night she heard the boots on the stairs in Travis's apartment. Her heart dropped into her stomach. She dug her foot into the ground so suddenly she almost catapulted herself out of the swing. She held tightly to the ropes. Even though it was a new moon and they were dressed all in black Maureen could clearly see the large group of men moving across the field in formation. She wondered how many of them there were. Was there a group in every sector? More than one? Maureen did the only thing she could do. She put her two fingers into her mouth and whistled as loudly as she could. Seconds later they were upon her.

"It's Maureen Baker!" one of them yelled before he shot her in the chest. Twice. And then shot her in the head.

It was over before it began. All the ranking Foodies in sectors eight through twelve were shot in their beds. If Jimmy had ever heard of them or seen their face, he made sure it was the last time. The Jasper security force destroyed every last crumb of food and slaughtered all the animals. Ginger sobbed and screamed, as they burned every last building and set fire to the crops. They hauled the survivors out to return them to Harvest. Angus, safe in the sling on Ginger's chest and oblivious to the catastrophe unfolding around him, nursed at his mother's breast. In the midst of the tragedy, one person, albeit a tiny one, continued to eat.

EPILOGUE: HARVEST

Beatrice Patterson awoke to the sound of her alarm clock. She turned it off and got out of bed. She took a quick, cold shower. She dressed in her pale green coveralls and went downstairs. In the kitchen, she got out a glass and filled it with H_2O. She placed her EZ Meal tablet on the kitchen table next to the glass and headed to the door to let out her Siamese cat, Cupcake.

She opened the front door and glanced down as Cupcake skipped past her and started down the steps. She noticed a little white cloth bag tied with a purple ribbon. Beatrice Patterson picked up the bag and glimpsed down the hall. Every single door had an identical cloth package just like hers. There was electricity in the air. Something was different today. She forgot about Cupcake and took the package back inside.

Beatrice brought the cloth bag to the kitchen table. She untied the purple satin ribbon. Inside the little cotton bag were three brown disks, about two inches in diameter. She picked up one of the brown disks and held it to her nose. It smelled sweet and spicy. A thought came to her from somewhere far away: Eat it. She remembered reading *Alice in Wonderland* as a young girl and the cake that read "Eat me." It hadn't ended well for Alice and the thought frightened and yet also excited her.

She had an overwhelming desire to put the little brown disk in her mouth. Was it even edible? Would it hurt her? Finally, she gave into the curiosity and took a bite. It was extraordinary. Beatrice Patterson chewed slowly. It was crunchy on the outside and chewy on the inside. She held the disk up to the light and watched it twinkle. There was something familiar about the disk. It tasted like a time and a place she knew but had never been. It tasted like something she had once known but had somehow forgotten. Then she uttered a nonsense word. "Christmas," she whispered. "It tastes like Christmas."

ACKNOWLEDGMENTS

I would like to thank everyone who encouraged me along the way, especially friends who asked me how the writing was going. Thanks to Haden for reading the manuscript and giving me comments early on. Thank you to my fabulous brother, Jonathan Smith, for doing the cover design for me. I'd like to thank my author friend, Jenn Brink, gave me a copy of her first novel, *Black Roses*. It gave me the courage to share my novel. Last but not least, I'd like to thank my husband, Stephen, for always welcoming wild-eyed up all night writing Emily.

ABOUT THE AUTHOR

Emily Echols lives in Fort Polk, Louisiana with her family where she bakes family recipes and writes. This is her first novel.